The Forsaken Man

Jim Sandford has been elected sheriff of Caldwell by a land-slide victory. Riding on a wave of popularity, it looks like Jim can do no wrong, even securing the attention of the prettiest woman in town. However, she has another admirer who isn't happy about the liaison and sets about to sabotage things for Jim.

Then Jim receives information that Wade Baxter is heading to Caldwell to settle an old score with the townsfolk who years ago set him up for a crime he didn't commit. Believing he has the backing of the menfolk, Jim confidently waits for his arrival. However, a series of events leads to the men of Caldwell abandoning their new sheriff one by one until Jim is forced to face Wade Baxter and his gang alone.

The Forsaken Man

Pete B. Jenkins

A Black Horse Western

ROBERT HALE

© Pete B. Jenkins 2019
First published in Great Britain 2019

ISBN 978-0-7198-3059-4

The Crowood Press
The Stable Block
Crowood Lane
Ramsbury
Marlborough
Wiltshire SN8 2HR

www.bhwesterns.com

Robert Hale is an imprint
of The Crowood Press

The right of Pete B. Jenkins to be identified as
author of this work has been asserted by him
in accordance with the Copyright, Designs and
Patents Act 1988.

Typeset by
Derek Doyle & Associates, Shaw Heath
Printed and bound in Great Britain by
4Bind Ltd, Stevenage, SG1 2XT

For my grandfather Sydney Henry Jenkins (1909-1980), who loved to read Westerns, from your grandson, who loves to write them

CHAPTER ONE

Stepping over the threshold of the sheriff's office then crossing the boardwalk, Jim Sandford leaned up against a post. A cigarette balanced precariously in the corner of his mouth, he glanced up the street one way then the other as he surveyed his new domain. Today was his first day as the newly elected sheriff of Caldwell in the proud state of Kansas, and he was relishing it.

Sure, he had trodden on a few toes to get the position, but then Sam Carrington, at fifty-eight years of age, had grown too old and complacent to be an effective sheriff, and should have surrendered his sheriff's badge several years ago.

Did Jim feel bad about winning the election and ousting his colleague and mentor? You bet he did, and what's more he had paid dearly for it by losing the older man's friendship and respect. Sam Carrington wouldn't have anything to do with Jim now, and that hurt, it hurt real bad.

It was Sam who had given Jim his first break in the

law enforcement business when as a twenty-two-year-old he was down on his luck. No job, and no prospects to speak of, Sam had offered Jim the role of deputy, and the young man had jumped at the chance to pin on a badge and finally be someone others would look up to. Sam had gently guided him through the early days, and with all the care and concern of a fatherly type moulded Jim into a fine lawman, so fine in fact, that the good citizens of Caldwell now preferred him as their sheriff over the older man who had unselfishly given them fifteen years of his life.

As he leaned against that boardwalk post, the smoke from his cigarette curling lazily towards the roof, he mused on how Sam would still have the job if he hadn't made such a mess of the Johnson ruckus a few months back. If he had brought about a satisfactory outcome there then Jim doubted anyone would have voted against Sam in the election. But the mistakes he made couldn't be overlooked, and so on the day the votes were counted Jim was swept to victory in a landslide, something that wounded Sam Carrington to his very core, and Jim suspected would continue to wound him for the rest of his life.

The Johnson family were the catalyst for that election victory. They had stirred up all and sundry to vote for Jim so it would be assured the older man would be put out to pasture, and Jim couldn't say he blamed them for it either. Hector and Ester Johnson's youngest son would probably still be alive if Sam Carrington had done his job right.

Billy Johnson had been a quiet, unassuming lad of
nineteen who wouldn't have lifted a finger to harm
so much as a fly let alone another human being. The
problem for Billy was, he had a nemesis who had
made it his mission since they were in school
together to persecute Billy every opportunity he got.
As kids, that entailed a bit of pushing and shoving
and the occasional black eye, but over the past few
years Jackson Sturge had stepped up his unjustified
vendetta against Billy to employ levels of violence
that had made Jim sick to his stomach.

Hector and Ester Johnson had laid a complaint
with Sam Carrington, of course, citing the fear that if
something wasn't done to rein Jackson in then there
would soon be a tragedy on their hands. Sam had tut-
tutted, assuring them that Jackson Sturge was merely
an over-exuberant lad who got a little carried away on
occasion. When the Johnsons challenged him over
his lack of professionalism, the sheriff had lost his
temper and told them they had molly-coddled young
Billy to the extent he was too soft, and that a few
hidings from Jackson Sturge would help make a man
of him.

Jim had been present on that particular occasion
and had quickly jumped in to remonstrate with the
older man on the Johnsons' behalf, reminding him
he was duty-bound to make sure the boy came to no
more physical harm at the hands of Jackson Sturge.

It was as if Jim had lit the fuse to a powder keg with
his remark. Sam Carrington almost hit the roof, his
face going scarlet with rage; he first swore at Jim, and

that in front of a woman, which he was never known to have done before, and then threatened him with dismissal if he were to ever challenge his authority in such a manner again.

The Johnsons walked out of the sheriff's office in disgust, leaving Sam and Jim eyeballing each other in stony silence until Jim turned on his heel and stalked after the Johnsons to commiserate with them over their inability to see justice done for their son.

Two weeks later Jackson Sturge beat Billy Johnson so savagely in the main street of Caldwell that he died less than forty hours later from the severity of his injuries. If Sam Carrington had done his job then Billy would not have had to die, and Jackson wouldn't have been convicted of manslaughter and put behind bars for twelve long years. After that, public opinion in the small town turned against Sam Carrington. Jim was asked to stand for the sheriff's office in the upcoming election, and now here he was, the top-ranking lawman in Caldwell.

It was a bitter sweet way to celebrate not only his first day as sheriff of Caldwell but also his thirtieth birthday. This would be the first time in eight years that Sam wouldn't stand him a drink down at the saloon to mark the anniversary of his birth. It saddened him to think the friendship was over, but then he had done everything he could to stop it from ending, short of pulling out of the race for sheriff that was.

A shout from the boardwalk outside the saloon yanked him free of his musings.

'Sheriff . . . Stacy Thomas is cutting up again.'

It was Fred Calder, barman at the saloon calling to him. Stacy was obviously blind drunk and throwing his weight around. Flicking the stub of his cigarette into the dust, Jim stepped down on to the street and with a heavy sigh headed in the direction of the saloon. If there was one thing the episode with Billy Johnson and Jackson Sturge had taught him it was to stamp on any form of bullying as soon as it reared its ugly head so as to prevent it leading to another fatality.

The batwings swished to and fro as Jim parted them and, stepping inside the Lonely Bull Saloon, he quickly cast his eyes around to assess the situation. One man was on the floor cradling his head in his hands while big Stacy Thomas held another by the throat with his left hand, forcing the hapless fellow to bend backwards in an unnatural fashion across the bar, while Stacy's balled up right fist was ready to strike him in the face.

'Let him go, Stacy!' Jim bellowed.

Stacy Thomas looked over his shoulder at the new arrival. 'He wuz laughin' at me, Jim,' he said, as if that was all the justification he needed to bust the man's head open.

'Doesn't matter.'

'I ain't gunna let him git away with it, Jim,' Thomas said adamantly.

Jim Sandford moved closer. 'I'm not going to tell you again, Stacy, let go of him or I'll have to arrest you.'

Stacy Thomas looked from Jim to his victim and then back to Jim again. 'He's got this comin' ter him I reckon,' then he struck him full in the face with that balled up fist.

Seeing the situation was likely to escalate despite his warnings, Jim decided to take action. Striding over to the bar, he delivered a stinging blow with the butt of his Army Colt to the back of Stacy's head, then stepped back to give the large man room to slump to the floor.

'Frank . . . Joe,' he said to a couple of men sitting at the nearest table to the action, 'help me get him over to the cells, will you?'

It was just over an hour later that Stacy came round. Rolling off the cot in his cell, he attempted to stand up despite the throbbing in his head, and his mood none the better for the pistol-whipping he had taken. 'Jim . . . Jim Sandford, yer get yer carcase in here, yer mangy polecat,' he bellowed.

Leaving the pile of paperwork he was working on, Jim left his desk and wandered through to the cells. 'Finally woken up I see.'

'No thanks ter yer.' Stacy probed his head gingerly with the fingers of his right hand, wincing with the pain when he made contact with the open wound. 'Why'd yer havta hit me with yer shootin' iron fer anyway?'

'Because you wouldn't leave that feller alone when you were told to. Believe me, I didn't want to have to resort to clouting you, but you left me with no other option.'

'Sam Carrington niva belted me on the head with his six-gun,' Stacy said bitterly.

'Sam Carrington ain't the sheriff any more. Besides, I aim to crack down on all the violence in this town, and doing things the way Sam used to just doesn't cut it.'

'I wish I'd niva gone an' voted fer yer now, Jim, an' that's the gospel truth. I niva woulda if'n I'd a known how yer'd turn out.'

'You toe the line and you won't get any more trouble from me,' Jim said firmly. 'Might be a good idea if you leave the drink alone too, you obviously can't handle the stuff.'

Stacy looked at him through the bars of his cell with contempt. 'Becomin' sheriff has gone ter yer head,' he said sullenly.

'There are gunna be some changes around here, Stacy,' Jim warned. 'If you don't like that then maybe it's time you made a life for yourself in some other town.'

'I wuz born an' raised in Caldwell,' Stacy said angrily. 'Ain't nobody gunna chase me away.'

'Then change your ways or it might just come to that.' Jim Sandford spun round and, walking through to the office, left his prisoner to digest his words.

CHAPTER TWO

The small bell at Brooks' Mercantile tinkled loudly as Jim's shaky hand closed the door to which it was screwed. He was nervous. He was very nervous. Harrison Brooks' beautiful daughter Julia was standing behind the counter a mere ten feet away, totally oblivious to the fact he was about to ask her to accompany him to the dance at the town hall this Saturday night.

The young lady in question looked up from her accounts book and smiled. 'Good morning, Mr Sandford,' she said sweetly.

Jim cleared his throat. Julia had to be about the most beautiful woman he had ever encountered in his life, and just looking at those sky blue eyes set in that gorgeous face set his heart pounding in his chest. He had never been confident with women, especially not the ones that possessed the class that Julia did. She was definitely way up there on her own. The only woman in town with long auburn hair that cascaded over her shoulders and down to the small of her back, the five foot six inch beauty was still inexplicably unmarried at the advanced age of twenty-four, a situation that Jim with all his heart was hoping to change.

The truth was, he had been in awe of her for the past eight years but had lacked the confidence to do anything about it until now. The sheriff's star pinned to his shirt made him feel he was finally someone of note, and so maybe Miss Julia Brooks would think so too. At least that was what he kept telling himself so he wouldn't chicken out of doing what he was about to do.

Those stunning eyes of hers were looking at him expectantly. She was obviously waiting for him to tell her what it was he wanted to buy so she could fetch it for him.

'Some tobacco please,' he stammered slightly, but managed to correct the problem by the time he asked for some matches as well.

'Congratulations on your appointment as sheriff,' she said as she busied herself cutting him some tobacco.

'Thank you.' He watched her as she went about her task, her long elegant fingers handling the knife she was using with unusual dexterity.

'Pa was saying at the supper table last night that it's long since time we had a younger man for sheriff.'

'Sam Carrington was a fine sheriff and served this town well,' Jim said quickly, not wanting her to think badly of the man he had once considered to be his best friend.

Her eyes left her task and searched his face for a moment, obviously trying to decide whether he was being sincere or not. 'Yes, of course he was,' she conceded, 'and he did serve us well. But nothing lasts forever, and a man's time to move on and make way for a younger one always comes in the end.'

Jim didn't say anything. He was torn between agreeing with her and remaining loyal to his former boss. One day, he figured, a younger man than he would come along and folks would be whispering behind his back about him being too old for the job. He just hoped when it happened people would remember how he never spoke a word out of turn about Sam Carrington.

'Is that all I can get you?' she asked when she had organized his purchases for him.

'Yes, thank you.'

Those sensational eyes were boring into him now, making him feel decidedly inadequate as a man. Placing some money on the counter he scooped up his goods and turned quickly so she wouldn't see his discomfort. He was halfway to the door when he came to his senses. If he could get himself elected as sheriff he could dang well ask a pretty girl to a dance or he was no man at all.

'Julia . . .' he turned back, heart hammering wildly, 'I wonder if you would allow me to escort you to the dance on Saturday night?'

There, he had done it, there was no going back now, he had made his intentions towards her clear and it only remained for her to either accept him or reject him.

Surprise registered in her blue eyes that left Jim wondering if it was because she thought him completely mad for thinking she would want to be seen on his arm, or whether it was because, like most folks in town, she thought of him as a confirmed bachelor.

'I think I would like that very much,' she said after his proposal had sunk in.

'That's fine . . . that's just fine. Yep, that's fine.' He had more than half expected her to turn him down and so now he was lost for words.

She giggled at his inability to string more than those few words together. 'What time will you pick me up?'

Think man think. His brain wouldn't work, he was so stunned she had said yes, so he just stared blankly at her.

She helped him out. 'It starts at six-thirty so how about coming for me at six-fifteen?'

'Six-fifteen is good. Yes, six-fifteen. Yes, six-fifteen is fine.' He was making a mess of this. The best thing would be to get out of the place as quickly as he could so she wouldn't think he was any more of an imbecile than she already did. 'I'll see you then,' he said, then made for the door lickety-split.

With the reality of what had just happened beginning to dawn on him, his spirits began to soar as he strode excitedly back up the street to the sheriff's office. Miss Julia Brooks, the most beautiful girl in the entire county, had just agreed to attend Saturday night's dance with him. He was going from strength to strength. The last few days had been like a dream come true, and he for one couldn't wait to see what the next couple of weeks held in store for him.

As Jim Sandford stepped through the door with Harrison Brooks' daughter on his arm all eyes in the room were on the young couple. Jim felt his chest swell with pride. Just a few short weeks ago he was next to being a nobody, but now as he navigated his date across the floor to the drinks table he could tell by the delighted smiles and head nods in his direction that people were pleased with their new sheriff, and with the fact that he had caught the eye of the prettiest girl in town.

All except Kurt Butler that was, if looks could kill then Jim would have been dead the moment he entered the room.

Butler had been trying to woo Julia Brooks for the past three years, and Jim had to admit not without a certain amount of success. She had accompanied him to several of these dances in the past as well as a few church picnics. There had been talk around town of the two taking things further, but Jim fancied he had just put an end to that. No wonder Kurt was glaring furiously at him.

Jim guided the girl to a chair, 'A glass of punch?'

'Yes please.'

Jim left her there for the time being and was busily employed in his task when Kurt Butler was suddenly at his elbow.

'I suppose you think you're something special now

you've got that star pinned to your chest,' Butler said sourly. 'Well you ain't nothing in my eyes, Sandford.'

'Sorry to hear that, Butler,' Jim said evenly, not wishing to cause a scene with his date sitting no more than eight or nine yards away.

'As if taking Sam Carrington's job from him wasn't enough, now you have to take my gal from me as well.'

'I was under the impression that Miss Brooks wasn't anybody's gal.'

'Well that's where you're wrong. I've invested a lot of time and money in her these past few years and expected to reap the rewards from it. But as soon as you got to pin that badge on she goes haring off after you and it's as if I never even existed.'

Jim looked up from his chore. 'You win some and then you lose some. You know that as well as I do, Butler.'

'I only lost cos I don't have a star pinned to my chest like you do,' Butler said, his anger at the situation beginning to show in his voice.

'Maybe you should run for office then,' Jim said, as with a drink in each hand he turned to make his way back to Julia. 'It worked for me.'

'This ain't over, Sandford,' Butler called after him. 'This ain't over by a long chalk.'

'What was that about?' Julia asked as Jim handed her a glass of punch.

'Kurt Butler isn't happy about you attending the dance with me. It appears he considers you to be his girl.'

'Well I'm not,' she said adamantly, and not without a certain amount of chagrin.

'He claims you've spent a lot of time with him in the past and so that gives him a claim on you.'

'We did spend a bit of time together,' she admitted. 'He seemed nice at first, but I stopped it when I discovered the foul temper he has. There is no way I want a man like that in my life.' She took a sip of her punch, her eyes watching him over the rim of her glass. 'I've never seen you lose your temper in all the years I've known you,' she said as soon as the glass left her lips. 'Why have you taken so long to ask me out?'

Jim sighed. 'I never thought I had a chance with you.'

'Well you do,' she said quietly, not looking at him this time but staring at the floor instead.

'I'm glad to hear that. I was beginning to think there was something wrong with me. After all, I'm thirty years old and I'm still not married.'

'You have been too reserved. If you had asked me before I would not have turned you down.'

He chuckled. 'Now you tell me. I could have done with being told that several years ago.'

'Well you know now and so the rest is up to you.'

Indeed it was, and Jim was determined to get his wedding ring on Miss Julia Brooks' finger now he knew she was open to the idea.

CHAPTER THREE

Climbing down from his mare, Jim flicked the reins around the hitching rail. Leaving the sorrel there, he made his way up the street towards the gunsmith. John Anderson had a new Colt .45 Peacemaker complete with hand-carved leather holster waiting for him to pick up, and he couldn't wait to see how that single action army revolver felt nestled in the palm of his hand. The Army Colt he packed now was getting decidedly long in the tooth, and Jim felt it wasn't becoming of a man of his office to be carrying it. The new weapon would go nicely with his new status.

He had been the sheriff of Caldwell for over a week now, and still folks were stopping him in the street to congratulate him. Several pledged their support to him, offering their services should the need arise. Larry Blake, Harry Clements, Jack Turnball, they were all good with a gun and would be an asset to Jim should trouble come calling.

'Morning, Jim,' John Anderson said brightly when Caldwell's sheriff stepped through the door of his shop. Reaching beneath the counter, he pulled out the new holster and six-gun and handed it to him. 'I think you'll be happy with this.'

Withdrawing the piece, Jim turned it over, studying it carefully before letting the butt nestle in his palm. That Colt Peacemaker felt like it belonged in his hand, its smooth grips inciting a shot of adrenalin to course through his veins as the thrill of what such a weapon was capable of struck him.

Anderson noticed the look of satisfaction on the young sheriff's face. 'You'll really be someone with that beauty sitting on your hip.'

Jim didn't doubt him for a second. He would be the envy of every man in town who packed a six-gun. This to him was the epitome of success. A weapon like this was a tool of the trade. Not some common shooting iron that a cowhand would be expected to own, but a quality, top of the line weapon made under the guidance of the best gunsmiths the Colt factory had to offer. With this on his hip, and as sheriff of Caldwell, Jim Sandford had finally arrived.

'It's the finest piece that's ever passed through my hands,' Anderson admitted. He grinned cheekily at Jim. 'Now all that remains to be seen is whether you're man enough to handle it.'

Jim took the joke in the manner in which it was intended. 'Outlaws beware, Jim Sandford is here,' and then he expertly twirled the pistol in his hand, first forwards and then backwards, much to the amusement and admiration of his onlooker.

'I bet you practised that long and hard before you

did it in public.'

Jim chuckled, 'More hours than I care to recall.'

'Jim,' Anderson said on a more sombre note, 'I want you to know that you can count on me for help if ever you need it. I'm more than handy with a gun myself, and I don't mind throwing my lot in with the law if the occasion demands it. Sam Carrington may have been a good man but he kept to himself far too much. If he had asked for help when he needed it then maybe he would still be sheriff of Caldwell. So I'm there for you if you ever need me.'

'Thank you, John,' Jim said appreciatively. 'It's good to know there are men in this town I can call on in a crisis, God forbid that it should ever come to that.'

After paying the gunsmith what he owed him, Jim strapped on his new acquisition and, vacating the store, stepped back out onto the street to see how having the fancy hardware that was nestled comfortably against his hip made him feel.

With the sun glinting spectacularly off the shiny metal of the .45 he sauntered down the street towards the sheriff's office, his head held high, the leather holster creaking pleasantly as the pistol moved ever so slightly with each step he took. Jim Sandford felt every inch the self-made man, and this new shooting iron just rounded things off nicely.

He bumped into Julia coming out of her father's mercantile and touching his hat smiled broadly at her.

'I enjoyed the dance the other night,' she said as

she returned his smile. 'You are a bit of a dark horse. Who knew that you were such a good dancer?'

'I have Ma to thank for that. She insisted I learn almost as soon as I could walk. Pa used to grumble about her teaching me though, reckoned too much dancing made a man soft. But Ma never paid him no mind. She just went right ahead teaching me how. She was the salt of the earth was my Ma.'

'That she was,' Julia agreed. 'And I have her to thank for raising you to be the man you are today.' She reached out and placed her hand on his bare forearm.

Jim caught a glimpse of someone lurking in the shadows of the boardwalk roof across the street and strained to make out who it was. A few seconds later that someone stepped forward into the sunlight and revealed his identity. Kurt Butler stood at the edge of the boardwalk glaring angrily in Jim's direction. He wasn't pleased to witness Julia's intimate touch, and he wasn't shy in showing it. With fists screwed up into tight balls of fury, he let Jim know he would be only too happy to unleash them on the town's new sheriff.

Jim didn't let on to Julia that Kurt Butler was watching them. He didn't want to concern her unnecessarily. Besides, he was fairly sure it was only him that Butler held the grudge against and not the pretty woman, so there was no point in alarming her.

'I do have my faults, Julia, which I'm sure you'll discover soon enough,' he said in answer to her comment. 'I just hope you'll still think highly enough of me to not send me packing.'

'I can't see that happening.'

It seemed to Jim that Miss Julia Brooks had put him on a pedestal, one that he feared he might come crashing down off one day soon if she was the fickle type of woman. Maybe that was how Kurt Butler started and finished in her estimation. Maybe his anger at being jilted was justified. Just maybe Julia Brooks couldn't hold on to her admiration for a man longer than a year or so.

'I must get back to the sheriff's office,' he said, suddenly feeling uncomfortable that she still had her hand resting on his arm.

She looked a little surprised. 'All right, I hope you will call on me soon.'

He just nodded and then moving past her strode with a sense of purpose towards the paperwork he knew awaited him on his desk.

That was poorly done, he thought to himself before he had gone more than forty yards. He wished he could turn around and go back and assure her everything was all right between them but she would be gone by now. He shouldn't have been so quick to assume she would be inconsistent in her feelings for him, but he just found it so hard to believe she would be interested in him after all these years of admiring her from afar and no indication from her until now that she liked him in return.

He had started this walk from the gunsmith to the sheriff's office in such high spirits, too. But now he felt more than a little deflated. Perhaps he should have given himself a few months in the job before he went running after Julia. He shouldn't really have any major distractions while he was learning the ropes so to speak. After all, the job came before his love life. Dang it, the job came before anything.

'Howdy, Jim,' Bart Newcomb, one of his two capable deputies looked up from his chore of cleaning a double-barrelled shotgun as his boss entered the office. 'Ready for an entire morning of paperwork?'

'Don't rub it in, pard. I reckon it's the worst part of being a sheriff.'

'You won't get any argument out of me there. It's one of the reasons I didn't run for sheriff myself.'

Plonking himself into a chair behind the desk, Jim dragged a stack of papers over to rest in front of him. 'And what were the other reasons?'

'Oh, the worry it brings, and having to be the feller who gives the speech at the Thanksgiving feast at the town hall every year. And, of course, you have to be polite to just about everyone, even the folks you just can't stomach.'

Jim looked across the desk at him. 'You have to be polite to everyone anyway, Bart.'

Bart Newcomb chuckled as he pushed the cleaning rod down the barrel, giving it a little twist as he did so. 'Nah, I'm just a lowly deputy. Folks don't expect so much from me, so I can get away with a whole heap more'n you can. Nope, I wouldn't want to be in your boots for anything.'

Jim signed the bottom of a form and slid it to the side before selecting another one. 'You ain't exactly filling me with a whole heap of confidence, Bart. You're supposed to be building me up, not tearing me down.'

'Far be it for me to do that to you, Jim. Nope, I reckon the good folks of Caldwell will do that to you soon enough, just like they did to poor old Sam Carrington.'

Jim felt a stab of guilt race through him. So even Bart felt Sam had been betrayed, and he obviously felt Jim was one of those who had betrayed him, too. He looked up as his other deputy Steve Reardon stepped over the threshold and entered the room. It was immediately obvious he wasn't wearing his badge. Jim's eyes stayed on him as he approached the desk, then opening his hand, Steve dropped the missing item onto the paper Jim had been working on.

'What's going on?'

'It's no good. I've tried to put it to one side and just concentrate on my job but I just can't.'

'Put what to the side?'

'The way you dealt to Sam.'

Jim sighed. So Steve thought he was a skunk for standing for office, too.

'Folks wanted a change, Steve,' he said in his defence.

'Not all folks.'

'No, I guess not all. But the majority did or they wouldn't have voted me in.'

'I can't work under you,' Steve said with bitterness straining his voice.

'That's your privilege, I guess.'

'Yep, it sure is.' He turned to leave but stopped before he had made it to the door. 'I hope you fall flat on your face,' he said bitterly. 'Sam Carrington has mighty big boots to fill, and I don't reckon you're man enough to fill 'em.' Then he was gone before Jim had the opportunity to respond.

'Do you want to quit too?' Jim asked Bart gruffly.

Bart Newcomb shook his head. 'I've got a wife and kids so I need the money.'

'But you figure I've done Sam wrong, too?'

'It doesn't matter what I think.'

'It matters to me.'

'I don't blame you for being ambitious. You'd been a deputy for a long time with no prospect of climbing higher up the ladder cos Sam was showing no inclination to retire.'

'And then the Johnson business happened.'

Bart nodded, 'And then the Johnson business happened, and we all knew Sam had finally failed not only the Johnsons but the town itself. That boy's death was preventable, and it was up to Sam to prevent it, but he didn't.'

'So you think I was right to stand against him?'

'Sam Carrington has served this community well for fifteen years. It was sad he had to go and spoil it by not giving a damn about that kid. You know a man's time to hang up his gun has come when he is either too old or lacking the fortitude to protect the weak and see justice done.'

'You haven't really answered my question.'

'You weren't wrong in standing, Jim, although there'll be plenty of folks who'd disagree with me, and Steve is obviously one of them. Loyalty is a wonderful thing until it is wrongly bestowed. You can't make a monumental mistake like Sam did and expect to remain in office.'

Jim breathed a sigh of relief. At least someone saw it the same way he did.

'You've made some enemies you didn't have before,' Bart continued, 'but I'm convinced you've got the goodwill of the majority or they wouldn't have voted for you as sheriff in such large numbers.'

'I do have the best interests of the people at heart,' Jim said, almost plaintively it seemed.

'I know you do, and you've got my support.'

'That means a lot to me, Bart.'

'We're left with the problem of who's gunna replace Steve though.'

Jim thought about it for a moment, 'How about Bill Matthews?'

'He's good with a gun but he's also fiery tempered. I reckon we can do without him stirring folks up unnecessarily.'

'Ted Harris?'

'With that gammy leg of his? We'd have to watch his back for him all the time.'

'I'll give it some thought during the week,' Jim promised. 'There's no rush anyway, I can't see anything cropping up that'll stretch you and me too much.'

Jim was glad he had at least one ally in Bart. The

man was level headed as well as experienced, and in a crisis about the calmest fellow Jim had ever come across. He knew he would be able to count on him whenever the chips were down.

CHAPTER FOUR

Ernest Snipes' face was as white as a sheet as he handed Jim the telegram. It had just come through at the telegraph office and he had hurried over to see the sheriff just as fast as his pudgy little legs would carry him.

Jim sat his coffee cup back down on the woodstove and took the slip of paper from the fellow's trembling hand. 'What's so all fired terrible that it's got you in such a tizzy, Ernest?'

'Read it and you'll see,' he answered breathlessly.

Jim Sandford glanced at the message. 'Who is Wade Baxter?'

'I was forgetting that you're too young to remember him. You wouldn't have been more'n about seven or eight when all that business blew up.'

'You'd better tell me what this is all about, Ernest,' Jim said, waving the piece of paper at him.

'Wade Baxter was about the meanest hombre that ever set foot in Caldwell. He terrorized just about everyone for just about anything.'

Jim considered what Ernest had just said for a moment. 'If that is true then why didn't Sam Carrington do something to stop him?'

'It was a few years before Sam became sheriff. We had a feller named Frank Davidson for sheriff then. It was him who stopped Baxter from getting his neck stretched.'

Picking his cup of coffee up again, Jim walked over to his desk and sat down. 'I've got the feeling this is gunna be a long story.'

Ernest found his own chair and, plonking himself down, launched right into it. 'Baxter was a bully who could pull iron faster than just about anyone alive, and he used that to get whatever he wanted. When he breezed into town we all thought he'd just stay for a few days and then breeze on out again, but for some reason he decided to stay.'

'And just where on God's green earth did this Baxter feller breeze in from exactly?'

'He never said and no one dared to ask him. But we all knew he was a mean one the moment he set foot in town. I remember him getting down from that big black gelding he rode and kicking Seth Harvey's poor old mutt for no other reason than the sheer joy of doing it. I knew then he was one ornery critter.'

Jim had known a few of those in his time, and they nearly always made the lives of those around them a living hell.

'Baxter was only in Caldwell three days before he killed his first man. Yancy Farrell didn't stand a chance against someone who lived by the gun like Wade Baxter did, and it was over nothing more than the fact Yancy had chosen to sit at the table Baxter considered to be his.'

'So Baxter killed Farrell and the sheriff did nothing about it?'

'He couldn't. You see, Baxter goaded Yancy into drawing first and in front of a room full of witnesses, so the sheriff could only rule it was done in self defence.'

Jim knew the sort. A gunfighter who hurled every insult imaginable at his intended victim until the fellow cracked, then losing his mind as well as his temper would rashly make a play for his gun, giving the gunfighter all the excuse he needed to kill him.

'After he got away with killing Yancy he just went from bad to worse. No pretty woman was safe from him manhandling them, and if any man objected he was liable to end up like poor Yancy. He killed three other men in the six months he lived in Caldwell.'

Jim glanced down at the piece of paper he still held in his hand. 'This says he's just been released from prison. If the men he killed drew on him first how did he end up doing time?'

The little man sighed. 'I ain't proud of my part in that but I reckon we were left with no choice. Baxter wouldn't leave and so we had to get rid of him one way or another before he killed half the male population of Caldwell.'

'Why do I get the feeling you're about to tell me something I'm not sure I want to hear?'

'Maybe because I am about to tell you something you don't want to hear.'

Jim frowned, 'Fire away then, Ernest.'

'Wade Baxter's behaviour got so bad that some of the men in town put their heads together to come up with a plan of getting rid of him.'

'You being one of those men I take it?'

Ernest Snipes nodded. 'I played my part in getting him locked up. I never thought I'd see the day he got out though. He was given twenty-three years hard labour so I honestly thought he would die there.'

'But he hasn't and now he's coming here for revenge?'

Snipes' normally pale face went even paler. 'He's going to kill everyone who had a hand in putting him away, I just know he will.'

'How exactly did you set him up so he got sent to prison?'

'We staged a fake robbery at the bank. Got the teller and bank manager and some of the townsfolk to claim it was Baxter who did it. It went to court, and even though Baxter swore he was innocent it didn't carry any weight with us saying we positively identified him.'

'And the jury believed your story over his?'

Snipes looked at Jim with fear in his eyes. 'The jury was in on it, too.'

'No wonder he's coming for you then,' Jim said matter-of-factly. 'I think I'd come for you if you set me up for twenty odd years hard labour for a crime I didn't commit.'

'It was more than that. We were so scared he would escape from custody that we formed a mob and one night we came down to the cells and dragged him out despite the deputies trying to stop us.'

'You planned to lynch him you mean?' Jim asked incredulously.

'You don't understand,' Ernest said in a plaintive tone. 'Wade Baxter was pure evil, and the only way we would have been truly safe from him was if he was dead.'

'Then why didn't you hang him?'

'Sheriff Davidson, who was off duty at the time, heard the commotion in the street and came down with two loaded sawn off double-barrels, one in each hand. He was the type of sheriff who fired first and asked questions later so we had to let Baxter go. If it hadn't been for Davidson, Baxter would be long dead, and we wouldn't be facing this problem now.'

'What a dang mess.'

'It sure is, but I just thought I'd better warn you,' Snipes said as he got up from his chair and pointed at the piece of paper in Jim's hand. 'My cousin sent me that. He reckons he spotted Baxter at a saloon he works in and overheard him telling some fellers he was playing cards with that he was coming here to settle a few scores.'

'Can I get you to wire your cousin and let us know when we can expect Baxter?'

Ernest Snipes shook his head. 'I've quit the telegraph office and I'm getting out of Caldwell today. I ain't going to be here when that mad man hits town, and that could be any time from today onwards. I'm going to head back East and see if I can get an office job in a city somewhere. Baxter won't be able to find me there.'

Jim stared long and hard at the message on that paper even after Ernest Snipes had left the sheriff's office, trying to make sense of it all. Wade Baxter was a fool if he thought he could come to Caldwell after all this time and wreak havoc unopposed. He was just one man against a whole town, and look what they did to him the last time he gave them trouble. Unless . . . just maybe this time he wasn't coming alone. Maybe he was bringing some help with him. If that was the case then the town was in trouble. In fact, they were in big trouble. With only one sheriff and one deputy to stand in their way death was surely coming to the normally sleepy town of Caldwell.

Pouring himself a cup of coffee and sitting down, Jim thought his options through. He needed to get the men of Caldwell behind him before Wade Baxter and his sidekicks made it to town. If they could present a united front then Baxter was less likely to start anything. What Jim really needed to do was call a public meeting and enlist the support of as many able-bodied men as he could, and he would need to do it quick, because he had no idea when Baxter was likely to turn up.

He sipped absentmindedly at his coffee. Yep, that was definitely the best plan of attack. Get everyone on side and armed to the teeth and Baxter would be sent scurrying off with his tail between his legs in no time. No matter how wild a man was, no matter the class of man who rode with him, he couldn't stand up to an entire town, and Wade Baxter would be no exception.

It seemed to Jim that he had been thrown in the deep end the moment he had taken on the role of sheriff. He couldn't remember Sam Carrington ever having to cope with something as big as this. Maybe he was being a little too harsh on the older man but he didn't think Sam would have been able to cope with it either. At least, not in his last two or three years in office anyway.

A large shadow darkened the light in the doorway, causing Jim to abandon his musings and focus his attention on the new arrival. 'Howdy, Jake,' he said with surprise, 'what brings you to my neck of the woods?'

Jake Westlake stood six foot three in his bare feet, and he had a massive girth to match his height. Not an ounce of fat resided on that gigantic frame; it was pure muscle from years of hard work breaking in his ranch. Forty-two years old but looking several years younger, he commanded the respect of every man who knew him, and not just for his impressive physique but for his exemplary character as well.

'Just come from the mercantile where I bumped into the little feller from the telegraph office,' he paused for a moment while he searched for a name. 'Dang it, I never could remember that feller's handle.'

Jim supplied the missing name for him. 'Ernest . . .

Ernest Snipes.'

'That's the feller. Anyway, he told me about the trouble that's heading this way and I wanted you to know I'll stand right alongside you if you need me to. There's no reason for you and your deputies to face this on your own.'

'I'm down to the one deputy now, Jake. Steve handed in his badge just this morning.'

'Well I'll be, and he's been a deputy for more years than I care to remember, too.'

'He didn't like the way I came by the sheriff's badge.'

'It was all done true and proper,' Jake said with surprise showing in eyes radiating a gentleness that was unusual in a man of his great stature.

'He felt I stabbed Sam in the back standing against him like I did.'

'Nonsense,' Jake retorted. 'That's what democracy is all about, and this great country of ours is built on it. I'm disappointed he would take that view of things.'

'Each to their own I suppose. But thank you for your support, Jake, it is much appreciated.'

'Wade Baxter won't get away with terrorizing this town again. Once was enough, and I can't see folks putting up with it again.'

'Nor can I, so I'm planning on holding a public meeting tomorrow night to let the whole town know Baxter's on his way here, and to enlist the help of as many men as possible. It's time to send a message to men like Wade Baxter that their type of conduct won't be accepted in this town.'

'I'll be there,' the big rancher promised, 'and I'll bring every one of my ranch hands with me.'

'That'd be just fine, Jake.'

Jim smiled to himself as the amiable man stepped back through the door of the sheriff's office to mount his horse and head back to his ranch. Jake Westlake was a no-nonsense character who was a good man to have on your side in a crisis. Jim felt better already knowing that the capable fellow would be standing right alongside him when Baxter and his bullies hit town, and it warmed his heart to know Jake would be bringing all eight of his ranch hands along with him, too.

CHAPTER FIVE

'Pa says there's trouble brewing for Caldwell,' Julia said anxiously as she and Jim sat on a blanket beside a bend in the river eating the picnic she had prepared especially for the occasion. 'He said this Wade Baxter who is coming here is about as bad as a man can get.'

'It's nothing for you to trouble yourself with,' Jim said gently, hoping to alleviate any fear she may be feeling. 'There were plenty of men who pledged me their support at the meeting the other night, so Caldwell will be ready for him when he arrives and we won't be tolerating any nonsense from him.'

'But Pa says he's not coming alone. He says he will have a gang of men with him.'

Jim smiled warmly at her. 'We have an even bigger gang of men in Caldwell. They aren't going to let

40

Wade Baxter cause any trouble.'

'I'd hate for anything to happen to you.' Her eyes were focused on an ant that was scurrying its way across the blanket. 'I have become quite fond of you these past few weeks.'

The comment made him smile. He had come a long way with the young woman in such a short time. Who would have thought it possible? He wouldn't have just two short weeks ago.

'I have become very fond of you, too,' he confessed. The truth was, he was in love with her and had been for more years than he cared to recall. But he wasn't ready to tell her that. Not just yet at any rate.

'I am glad about that.'

'Anyway, to put your mind at rest, I'm not planning on letting anything bad happen to me, Julia.'

'You may not be able to stop it.'

'Sam Carrington was sheriff for fifteen years and nothing happened to him.'

'Sam Carrington didn't have to contend with a man like Wade Baxter.'

He was obviously not going to persuade her that he was going to be perfectly all right, so he decided to change the subject instead. 'How is the mercantile doing?'

'It's doing very well. Pa says we will soon have enough money saved so we can move to a larger house. He has his eye on a two-storey house at the south end of town. He says it will be more in keeping with our social status.'

Jim chuckled at the comment.

'What's so funny, Jim Sandford?' she asked crossly.

'You and your pa. What does it matter what house you live in? Just so long as it's warm and dry is all that matters.'

'It matters to Pa,' she said defensively. 'He's always wanted to amount to something, and now that he finally has he wants the world to know it.'

'And they'll know it by the house he lives in?'

She blushed. It did all sound rather snobbish. But her pa was inextricably bound up in that world of those who were considered to be successful and he would do anything within his power to make sure he stayed bound up with them.

'I reckon a man's amounted to something when he lives his life by the golden rule, Julia. The amount of money or possessions he has doesn't mean a thing if he's mean spirited towards others.'

'Yes, of course.'

Jim wasn't sure if she was being sincere or not. Perhaps she was just agreeing with him to keep the peace. He couldn't expect to get her to see that not having money didn't mean a person wasn't worth anything, at least not straight away. She was a product of her upbringing, and so for her success was having all the trappings of life, because that was what she had been taught from the moment she had been born. He would have to bring her around to the right way of thinking slowly and gently, otherwise he risked destroying this relationship before it really even got off the ground.

Jim had to admit he did have dreams of his own

though. He didn't want to be sheriff of Caldwell for the rest of his life. One day he would like to own a little spread somewhere, it didn't have to be around here, maybe somewhere the winters were warmer and the summers a little wetter so the grass would grow all year round. A good-sized house where he could raise a brood of children without cramming them all in would be nice, too. Whether or not that would be an ambition that would pass muster in the sight of Julia and her father, Jim did not know just yet, but that was what had been on his mind for quite some time now and he didn't think it was going to change any time soon.

'You've gone very quiet all of a sudden,' she said after several minutes had elapsed and he was still lost in his thoughts.

'I was just thinking about the future,' he confessed.

She smiled at him in a way that only she could. 'And was I in that future?'

'I think that rather depends on you. I can plan a future but I can't force someone to share it with me.'

Julia was busily employed plucking petals from a wildflower she had picked. 'I don't think you would need to force any woman to follow where you lead, Jim Sandford.'

She was sending all the right signals, but Jim had seen plenty of women do that to smitten men in the past, only to witness them get cold feet when push finally came down to shove. Some women could be surprisingly fickle creatures, and as yet he didn't know if Miss Julia Brooks fitted into that category or not, but he figured if she did then she would start showing her true colours soon enough.

The rest of the afternoon was passed pleasantly enough, Julia proved to be a good conversationalist, which Jim appreciated. He had never cared for the sort of woman who only knew how to talk about frivolous matters, such as the latest dress fashions, or what young couples were currently stepping out together. Julia Brooks had a lively, intelligent, and enquiring mind, and Jim found the topics she chose to discuss both stimulating and enlightening.

'Thank you, Jim, I had a wonderful time,' she said with what appeared to be sincerity when he dropped her off at her house later on that afternoon.

'So did I.'

'We must do it again soon.'

He nodded. 'I would like that very much.'

She opened the door to the house and, stepping inside, turned and gave him a smile before closing the door, leaving him standing there on the Brooks' front porch revelling in his newfound popularity. He had come such a long way in such a short time, but he was astute enough to know he owed it all to the tin star that was pinned securely to his shirt.

Ethan Drake was a small wiry man in his early forties who didn't command much in the way of attention in Caldwell. He owned a smallholding a few miles out of town on land that yielded little in the way of profitable crops, but he was a hard worker who somehow managed to scratch out a living to keep his wife and six kids fed and clothed. His features wore the perpetual look of a troubled man, the uncertainties of life he carried around with him etched deeply on his prematurely lined face. As he stepped across the threshold of the sheriff's office that face showed the strain his worries were placing him under to an even greater degree than usual, and it would have taken a callous person indeed not to have noticed.

'Hello, Ethan,' Jim said, as he placed his cup of coffee down on the oak desk in front of him and waited for the man to state his business.

'Howdy, Sheriff,' Drake slowly worked his battered wide-brimmed hat around in a circle with his big work-roughened hands. 'I've got a problem I'm hopin' you can fix for me.'

'I'll certainly try my hardest to if it's within my jurisdiction, Ethan. How about you tell me exactly what this problem is.'

Ethan Drake couldn't bring his eyes up to look at Jim. He wasn't sure how the new sheriff was going to take what he was about to tell him.

Jim sensed his discomfort. 'How about you pull up a chair and take the weight off your feet,' he signalled to the wooden chair on the other side of the desk.

Dragging the chair out Ethan meekly sat himself down. 'I'm truly sorry to bother you with this, Sheriff, and normally I wouldn't, but for the fact that without water I'd have to walk off my land, and then where would I be?'

'You've got some sort of a problem with water?' Jim asked, wondering how in the blazes that could possibly involve Caldwell's sheriff.

Ethan Drake nodded his greying head. 'It's stopped running to my place.'

It took a moment or two for the comment to sink in. 'How can it have stopped running to your place . . . there hasn't been a drought?'

'It's stopped running to my place because Jake Westlake has stopped it from running to my place.'

'Why has he done that?'

'On account of some new-fangled dam he's built up near his ranch house.'

Jim's brain processed the piece of information. Jake Westlake had obviously built a dam on his ranch and had diverted the stream that normally ran down through Ethan's property so that the water it carried went to his dam instead.

'So there isn't any water coming down as far as your holding?'

'Nary a drop.'

'Have you spoken to Westlake about this?'

'Saw him 'bout it just this mornin'.'

'And what did he have to say?'

'Just told me he'd do whatever he wanted to do with the water that flowed through his ranch.' Ethan looked at Jim through the saddest brown eyes he had ever seen. 'All my crops are gunna die unless I can get water to them real soon. Some of them are startin' to wilt already.'

'And no water for the livestock and house as well?'

Drake shook his head.

'If I recall correctly you have a legally signed water right, Ethan.'

'That's right, I do. But Jake Westlake doesn't care about water rights.'

'Well he has to, that's the law.'

'The way I see it, Jake Westlake thinks he's above the law.'

'Nobody is above the law, Ethan, not even me.'

A glimmer of hope sprang into Ethan Drake's clear blue eyes. 'So you'll see him about it?'

'I'll ride on out there right now. You need that water and you need it pronto or you're gunna face financial ruin. I won't stand by and watch that happen to you, Ethan, you have my word on that. You'll have that water flowing back down past your house before nightfall.'

Ethan Drake looked close to breaking down. The relief was so great that a tear even slipped from an eye and slid lazily down his cheek. 'God bless you, Sheriff,' he said with sincerity. He got up from his chair and with a completely different demeanour than the one he had walked in with, departed for his farm.

CHAPTER SIX

Jim rode up to the Westlake ranch house feeling that this was nothing more than a storm in a teacup. He had always found Jake Westlake to be a more than reasonable man. This business between him and Ethan Drake over water must be little more than a misunderstanding; surely it was nothing more than that.

Climbing down from his mare, he loosely wrapped the reins around the post at the front gate and walked up the path to the front door with high hopes of reaching an agreement that would be acceptable to all parties.

It was Bethany Westlake, Jake's wife who answered the door. 'Why, Jim Sandford,' she said with a surprised smile, 'how delightful to see you out our way.'

'It's nice to be here, Mrs. Westlake,' Jim responded, touching the brim of his Stetson in greeting. 'I was wondering if it would be possible for me to see Jake for a few minutes.'

The smile faded somewhat. 'Are you here on official business?'

Jim nodded.

'Nothing serious I hope?'

He attempted a smile. 'I reckon it's nothing that can't be put right with a quick chat, Mrs. Westlake.'

'Well, he's up at the new dam,' she stepped clear of the door and walking down the steps and along to the path as far as the gate pointed to a spot on the horizon. 'If you ride in that direction you'll come to the dam soon enough. It's not much more than a fifteen-minute ride.' She looked at him with a searching eye, as if she knew that the conversation he was about to have with her husband was going to be more than just a little chat that would put everything right.

Pulling the reins free of the post, Jim put his foot in the stirrup before swinging himself into the saddle. 'I'm much obliged to you, Mrs. Westlake,' he said as he seated himself comfortably, then moved off quickly before she could ask him any questions he might not feel he could answer.

The Double J Ranch was a profitable spread and so named because Jake's father's name had been Jake as well. The older man had been so chuffed to be presented with a son at the grand old age of fifty-two that he had named the previously unnamed ranch the Double J to let everyone know that it was going to be as much his son's heritage as it was his own. When Jake senior had passed on a few years back and the ranch had come into the younger man's sole possession he had kept the name alive out of love for his deceased pa.

It was good land boasting rich fertile soil, and grew an abundance of grass so long as the rain kept falling at regular intervals, which it normally did. But it lacked free flowing water, the only creek running through the property being the currently disputed one that Jake Westlake had diverted. That meant the cattle that were the mainstay of the whole business needed to walk long distances to find water, causing parts of the ranch to be abandoned for grazing except in the wetter winter months. Jim figured this new dam Jake had constructed had something to do with rectifying that problem.

Jake Westlake appeared to be every bit as surprised to see Caldwell's new sheriff ride up as his wife had been if the expression on his face was anything to go by.

'Howdy, Jake,' Jim said cordially.

'Well howdy there yourself, Jim, what brings you all the way out to the Double J?'

Jim Sandford's eyes took in the new dam with one great circular sweep before he answered Westlake's question. 'This does,' he said in a no-nonsense fashion.

Westlake guessed from the lawman's tone that he was not happy about the project. Laying down the hammer and nails he had been using to construct a water race, he straightened up and looked the man he considered to be his friend in the eye. 'Something's on your mind. Might be best if you just come right out with it.'

Jim nodded towards the vast expanse of water. 'It looks more like a small lake than a dam to me.'

'It certainly ended up being a lot bigger than I originally intended it to be.'

'It's going to take a whole heap of water to fill it all the way to the top and keep it filled.'

'Yep, that's why I've got the creek feeding into it.'

'You're stealing water from your neighbours, Jake,' Jim said plainly.

Jake Westlake's sky blue eyes took on a look of hurt. 'I've never stolen anything in my life, Jim.'

'This water belongs to everyone downstream just as much as to you.'

'I see. That sodbuster Drake has been complaining to you, has he?'

'And with good cause.'

'You ain't gunna tell me you're siding with him now are you?'

'Ethan Drake needs water just as much as you do, Jake. In fact, probably more than you do. Without it he'll be ruined.'

Westlake spat contemptuously onto the ground at his feet. 'He's wasting his time on that barren piece of dirt he calls a farm. He should have packed up and moved on years ago.'

'But he hasn't, and he doesn't have to simply because you want him to. He has every right to farm that little piece of barren dirt as you call it, and he has every right to his share of this water as well. He does after all own water rights.'

'The hell he does,' Westlake said, his pulse rate

beginning to quicken. 'My pa was here long before Ethan Drake was even born. The Westlake family ain't some Johnny-come-latelys demanding what belongs to those who have been here decades before them.'

'I figure no one owns water, Jake. It falls from the sky by the grace of God for the use of all men, not just a privileged few.'

'Well he'll just have to get over it because I've spent a lot of money on this dam and I ain't about to abandon it to please the likes of a dirt farmer like Ethan Drake.'

'Mr Drake ain't asking you to abandon it. He just wants you to let enough water slip by so he can water his crops and livestock. Now that ain't too much to ask is it?'

Jake Westlake's normally friendly face clouded over with anger. 'I need every single drop of the water flowing from that creek to get water down to the rest of the ranch. If I can get water to the parts that don't have any I can graze them all year round, and that mean's almost doubling the number of beef I can carry. I'm a businessman as well as a rancher, Sheriff, and I'll be hanged if I'm gunna let that sod-buster destroy my plans to increase the profits on the Double J.'

'And as sheriff around these parts I'll be hanged if I'm gunna let you force Ethan Drake and his family off their land, simply because you've become too greedy to care about anyone or anything except your precious profits.' There, it was said, and as soon as it had left Jim's mouth he knew his relationship with Jake Westlake was never going to be the same again.

Jake Westlake stood there without saying a word, he merely stared up at Jim as if he would like nothing more than to drag him off his mare and lay into him with his fists.

'I'm heading down to Ethan Drake's now and I'm giving it until the sun goes down to see water running in that creek beside his house or I'll be back with my deputy and we'll use dynamite on this lake so it'll never hold water again.' He gave it a moment or two for his threat to sink in. 'There's enough water flowing in that creek so you can both have a share in it. You don't need it all.'

Wheeling his horse around, he dug his heels in to encourage the mare to break into a canter. The truth was he wanted to get away from the Double J Ranch and Jake Westlake and his high and mighty attitude just as quickly as he could. This entire business had left a decidedly sour taste in his mouth that wasn't going to disappear in a hurry, and it wouldn't at all if he stuck around here and listened to anymore drivel from the man he had always believed considered every man his equal, but now knew didn't.

Jim hung around Ethan Drake's homestead just long enough to see the water begin to flow again.

'I can't thank you enough, Sheriff,' Drake said, his eyes misting over as the creek began to chuckle once more with the sound of water tumbling over rocks. 'It means everything to the missus and me this place does, and what you've just done for us allows us to stay on here.'

'Just did my job is all, Ethan, nothing more nothing less. You are entitled to your share of this water and Jake Westlake has to respect that fact whether he likes it or not.'

Ethan frowned. 'I can promise you he won't like it.'

'Such as the case may be, but he has to go along with it anyhow.'

'I want you to know that if there's anything I can do for you, Sheriff, anything at all just let me know. I'll not turn you down no matter what it is.'

'Thanks, Ethan.' Jim couldn't think what use the fellow would possibly be to him but the sentiment was appreciated nonetheless. He looked up at the sky and noticed the sun wasn't too far from dropping down over the line of hills in the distance. 'I'd best be heading back to town before it gets dark, all the best with getting that crop watered tomorrow.'

'Oh, I'll be doing that tonight. It's always best to water the plants when it's cooler rather than in the heat of the day. Besides, they've gone without water for too long already, so the sooner I give them a good drink the better.'

With a smile and a nod, Jim turned the mare's head in the direction of Caldwell and with a quick dig of his heels soon had the creature trotting along comfortably.

CHAPTER SEVEN

Jim had just checked the door to the jewellers to make sure it was locked. Harold Dobson was notorious for finishing work and then forgetting to lock the door before heading home for the evening. At seventy-eight years of age he was too old to still be working but he lived for the interaction with his customers and dreaded the day he would have to close the doors to his little shop forever. The problem was, the older he got the more forgetful he got, and so Jim had to check that his shop door was secured every night to prevent an opportunist thief from paying him a visit. He had just left Dobson Jewellery store behind when a movement up a darkened side alley caught his attention.

'Who's there?' he called out, thinking it was unusually late for someone to be out and about, especially in a rarely frequented alleyway.

There was no answer even though Jim was certain he saw something move. He decided to check it out and see if someone from the saloon had imbibed a little too much and staggered into the alley. They could sleep it off in one of the cells for the night, where they would be safer than crashing around amongst the trash and rubble of the neglected alley.

He was not more than four or five yards into the alley when he felt a crushing blow against his left shoulder. Despite the pain it generated, he was still alert enough to realize that whoever had delivered it had been aiming for his head. Spinning around, he could just make out a dark figure in front of him, a club of some description raised above its head ready to strike again.

Instinctively Jim placed his gun hand in front of his face to protect it and yelped loudly as every bone in that hand was jarred by the agonizing impact. Someone meant business, and unless he defended himself he was going to wind up dead. Dropping his shoulder, he charged blindly, hoping to make contact with the torso of whomever it was who had it in for him.

He was instantly rewarded by a loud grunt, which was followed by a thump as his attacker's body was slammed against the side wall of the jeweller's. Quickly working his left hand around to pull his Colt clear of his holster, he poked it into the soft belly of his assailant and cocked back the hammer with his thumb.

'Go ahead,' he barked angrily, 'give me all the reason I need to pull the trigger and put a hole in your cowardly hide.'

Jim's adversary froze. 'Don't shoot,' he said in a

trembling voice.

'Drop that dang club and I won't.'

The lump of wood thudded to the ground.

With his pistol still pushed deep into the folds of belly fat, Jim backed his prisoner out into the street to get a better look at him by the light of the nearest gas lamp.

'Kurt Butler,' he said in disgust when he had positively identified him, 'I should have known. You just can't handle me courting Julia Brooks can you?'

'I wanted you out of the way, Sandford. I was doing fine with Julia until you pushed your nose in where it wasn't wanted.'

'It's wanted by Julia, I can assure you.'

Butler raised his fist to strike, so Jim twisted the barrel of his six-gun against his stomach to remind him it was still there.

'You're a brave man when you've got a gun in your hand.'

'Braver than the feller who ambushes a man in a dark alley with a club in his hand, I can assure you of that, Butler.'

'I'll get you, Sandford. I swear I'll get you one day soon.'

'Well it ain't gunna be tonight cos you're spending it in a cell.' He prodded the man with the barrel of his six-gun several times with unnecessary but deeply satisfying savagery. 'Now get your mangy carcase moving and don't try anything on because I'm just itching to plug you with what I've got in all six chambers.'

'What have we got here?' Deputy Bart Newcomb said as Jim marched his prisoner through the door of the sheriff's office.

'Mangy polecat tried to jump me in an alley. Hit me with a wooden club. Twice mind you. It's a miracle I ain't got a broken skull.'

'It's so thick I don't think much of anything'd penetrate it,' Bart said jovially.

'Har de har har, Bart,' Jim said without taking offence. 'Now could you get your lazy butt up from my chair and grab the keys to the cell. This feller is going to be paying us an extended visit.'

'You ain't keeping me in here for long, Sandford,' Butler rasped furiously.

'I'll be keeping you in here for just as long as I care to, Butler. You tried to kill me back there and that's gunna earn you a charge of attempted murder.'

'You wait till my pa and brothers hear about this. You'll wish you never tangled with me then.'

'If they give me any trouble then they'll be joining you in here, making it one big happy jailbird family.'

Bart Newcomb couldn't help but laugh at the comment. 'I reckon there's a song in that somewhere.'

'You'll keep, too, Newcomb,' Butler said resentfully.

'It'll be a cold day in hell when you and the Butler clan get the better of Jim and me.' He walked back through to the sheriff's office with Jim, ignoring the shouted threats from the incarcerated man.

'I don't know what Julia ever saw in that feller,' Jim

said as he held his swollen hand next to the gas lamp to inspect it.

'Glory be!' Bart exclaimed when he spotted the state of the injured member, 'what in the name of Sam Hill happened to that?'

'Butler swung a club at me and I stopped it with my hand.' He screwed up his face. 'I know, I know, it sounds like a silly thing to do but it all happened so quickly there wasn't time to do anything else.'

'You'd best go and bang on Doc Turner's door and get it seen to. I don't think it'd be a good idea to leave it until morning.' He waved his hand towards the open door when he realized his boss was reluctant to disturb the good doctor at this late hour. 'That's what the old buzzard gets paid for, and he charges handsomely for it too so don't you go feelin' bad about getting his old bones out of bed. That hand needs seeing to, I tell you.'

Jim nodded. 'Perhaps I will then.'

'It'd be the wise thing to do.'

Jim could hear the old man grumbling as he descended the stairs of his two-storey house to answer the door. He might charge handsomely but this was obviously one occasion when he didn't care to be disturbed.

'Sorry to bother you at this time of night, Doc,' Jim apologized when the medical man opened the door and peered out into the gloom to see who it was, 'but I've seriously hurt my hand and I didn't think I should leave it until the morning before I got you to take a look at it.'

'Well you'd better come inside where I can get a better look at it, young man,' Turner said with barely concealed displeasure.

'It's pretty busted up I'm afraid.'

Turner led him over to a lamp that was spluttering away on a small table and, taking up the hand in his own, inspected it carefully. 'Does this hurt?' he asked, squeezing Jim's palm a little.

Jim winced, 'Like blazes,' he admitted.

'Well it appears you've broken at least two of the metacarpals. All I can do for you is strap the hand up as tight as you can bear and hope nature comes to the party and knits them back together. You won't be able to use that hand at all for several weeks though.'

Jim nodded. 'Do whatever you think best, Doc.'

Twenty minutes later he left Doc Turner's house with his hand heavily bandaged. It was a shame it had to be his gun hand but that was the way it had panned out so there was nothing he could do about it now. He would have to pay the gunsmith a visit tomorrow and see if he had a left-handed holster he could buy. Kurt Butler had a lot to answer for, and Jim was determined he would, and in front of a court of law at that. Butler's family might kick up a ruckus over it but there was no way Jim was going to turn a blind eye to such a blatant disregard for a duly elected sheriff; if he did, then it would encourage other young hotheads in Caldwell to follow suit, and then neither he nor Bart would be safe from an unprovoked attack.

This was certainly not the way he had wanted to start his tenure as sheriff, and he was determined that it wouldn't be the way he carried it on. Sam Carrington had been a man of standing in Caldwell for several years, but towards the end he had lost the respect of too many people and that had led to his downfall. His mistake had been to become complacent. Trading on his years as the top lawman in Caldwell, he had come to believe that just a word from him was enough to bring any wayward soul back into line, when in fact sometimes it required a much firmer hand to bring about the desired result.

Jim had learnt from the experience of the older man and wasn't about to walk down that particular path. If he had to bang a few heads together to make troublemakers see sense then that was exactly what he would do. The good citizens of Caldwell would thank him for it in the long run, especially when they saw that his methods brought about results. Come next election time he fully expected to be returned to office with an even bigger portion of the vote.

Julia made a fuss of Jim when she saw the bandaged hand when he stopped off at the mercantile to see her the next day. Taking the injured hand gently in her small ones, she looked lovingly at him. 'I can't believe Kurt would do this to you. I knew he had a temper, but from what you've just told me about the attack it sounds as if he was out to kill you.'

'That's the way it appeared to me,' Jim agreed.

'Will he stand trial for it?'

'That's my intention.'

'Good for you. Maybe at last he'll learn to treat people with respect instead of believing they have been put here for his convenience.'

'I don't know if a man like Butler ever learns from his mistakes, Julia. But he's certainly going to be punished for what he's done.'

'Most folks would be behind you all the way where Kurt is concerned,' Julia admitted. She shot an anxious glance at him then that let him know that what she was about to say next wasn't going to be what he wanted to hear. 'But I think quite a few are going to disagree with how you handled that dispute between Jake Westlake and Ethan Drake.'

'I don't see how they could,' he said a tad defensively. 'Ethan Drake has a right to draw water from the creek that runs through his smallholding, and Jake Westlake knows it. He can't take all the water for himself and leave none for Ethan. It's not right morally, ethically, or legally for that matter.'

'I don't think most folks think long and hard as to whether it's legal or not. They consider Jake Westlake to be a man of honour and if he wants to take more water so he can increase the number of head of cattle he runs on the Double J then that's all right by them.'

'It ain't all right with Ethan Drake and his wife.'

Her pretty face creased up in a frown. 'Ethan Drake isn't exactly a popular man in Caldwell, Jim.'

'And why is that?'

She hesitated.

'It wouldn't be because he's a poor man would it?'

She sighed. 'He rarely patronizes any of the businesses in town. Not like Jake Westlake does anyway.'

'That'd be because he has to make do with what he's got. He doesn't have spare cash floating around that he can spend in town on luxury items, Julia.'

'Pa says he is a little simple,' she said defensively.

'The Ethan Drake I know isn't simple. He's polite and unassuming, which from what you've just told me obviously causes people to consider him to be inferior.'

'Jake Westlake just has a lot more going for him.'

'Yep, like eight thousand acres of prime grazing land compared to Ethan's tiny piece of dirt. I'm surprised at you, Julia. I never took you for being a snob.'

'I'm not!' she said despairingly. 'It's just that I know whom I like and whom I don't.'

'But your likes and dislikes appear to be based on the size of a man's bank account.'

'I think you are being very unfair to me, Jim,' she said coldly.

'Am I? Or is it more that you don't like your family's values being challenged?'

Her breathing was coming more rapidly now than when they had first begun the conversation and it could only be because she was very upset at what he had just said.

'I think your conduct has been very un-gentlemanly,' she said with a trembling voice. 'I don't want to speak to you while you are behaving this way.'

'Then I will leave you to get on with your day,' he said stiffly, and without another word passing between the two of them, he turned and strode out of the store a disappointed man.

CHAPTER EIGHT

Julia wasn't at church the following Sunday, making it four days in a row that he hadn't seen her. She was obviously still annoyed with his comment about being a snob and wasn't ready to forgive him yet. No matter. He was sure she would get over it before next Sunday rolled around and they would be sitting beside each other again as they listened to the sermon.

'Hello, Jim,' a very pretty young woman said as he filed past the last pew towards the door of the church.

Jim Sandford cast his eyes in the direction the voice had come from. Ruth Matheson was sitting beside her mother in all her Sunday finery looking every inch the eligible maiden.

'Hello, Ruth,' Jim answered, thinking she looked a whole lot more grown up than the last time he had seen her, and a whole heap prettier, too.

'Congratulations on your appointment as sheriff.'

'Thank you.' He began to shuffle along behind

the long line of people heading for the door.

'You won't stay and talk a while?'

She had sounded a little disappointed. Maybe his turning his back on her and walking away had come across as rude. 'If that would be all right with you and Mrs Matheson then I would like that very much,' he said, hoping to redeem himself in her eyes.

'Ma and I would like to catch up with you for a few minutes. We haven't seen you in ever so long.'

He plonked his solid frame down beside her. 'Some folks would be over the moon to be able to say that.'

'They wouldn't be folks I would care to be in the company of then.'

He studied her face as closely as etiquette would allow and came to the conclusion that she had blossomed into a very beautiful woman indeed.

'I am having a twenty-first birthday party out at the ranch next Saturday afternoon,' she said cheerfully. 'I would be very pleased if you would attend.'

'I must admit I'm not much of a one for parties, Ruth.'

'I know. You never did like socializing, did you?'

He shook his head.

'Still, I would be sad if you weren't there.'

He was aware of the fact that Miss Ruth Matheson had harboured a long-standing crush on him ever since she was fifteen years old and he had driven her home in their family buggy after a dance as a favour to her father. Mr Matheson had taken rather ill and had been obliged to spend the night in town at his sister's place, but was determined his daughter should return home to let her mother know he would be all right and not to worry.

The young girl had been a veritable chatterbox on the journey home, asking him all sorts of questions, some a little too personal for him to answer truthfully. But she had been pleasant enough company, and when they had arrived at the ranch and he had untied his gelding from the buggy and was about to return to town, she suddenly stole a quick kiss and then high-tailed it into the house before he could see the colour rising in her cheeks. She had blushed nearly every time they had crossed paths after that, and it was obvious to all and sundry that she held a candle for him. But the girl he was looking at now was no longer that, she was most definitely a woman, and a highly desirable one at that.

'Since you put it like that then I guess I don't have much choice.' He smiled to let her know the invitation would be much more of a pleasure than a burden.

'That will be wonderful. I can't remember the last time we spoke.'

Neither did he. In fact, he couldn't even remember the last time they had seen each other. It must have been well over two years ago. 'Now that you mention it, nor can I.'

She was silent for a moment and he could see she was thinking hard about it. 'It was a few weeks before I left to go and live with my aunt in Boston I think. You changed the wheel on my gig because it had come loose. Do you remember that?'

Now that she had mentioned it he did. He had just come out of the sheriff's office and saw her and the gig heading down the street with that wheel wobbling all over the place. He had shouted out to her to pull up and then had changed it for the spare right there on the spot. It was then she had told him, and very sadly too he seemed to recall, that she was leaving for Boston in a few weeks time. 'Yes, I do remember changing that wheel for you,' he admitted. 'I always considered it a pleasure to be able to do something for you, Ruth.'

She blushed then, in much the same way he remembered she used to as a girl, but with her now being unmistakably a woman, and a beautiful one at that, the result made a bigger impression on him than it ever had before.

'I must warn you that there will be dancing,' she said when the colour had faded from her cheeks, 'and I will expect you to dance at least once with me.'

He chuckled. 'I think I can manage that. But I doubt you'll ever want to dance with me again afterwards, because I can assure you my dancing skills have not improved with the passage of time.'

'I'll take my chances, Jim. Just promise me you'll be there at two o'clock next Saturday afternoon.'

He got up from the pew and smiled down at her. 'Wild horses wouldn't keep me away.'

His encounter with Julia Matheson stayed with him for the rest of the day and well into the next. She had been such a delightful young girl he seemed to remember, kind to everyone no matter what their personal or financial circumstances, and generous to a fault. She never bore a grudge or made anyone feel they were beneath her. Her sunny disposition had made her a favourite of so many folks in Caldwell and he hoped against hope that adulthood hadn't robbed her of any of those qualities.

He thought about the unpleasant time he was forced to tell her there could never be anything between them. She would have been about seventeen or thereabouts and he nine years her senior. She just couldn't understand that he was too old for her and had cried when he had to gently but firmly insist she look for a husband elsewhere. She had seemed merely a child to him back then, a sort of little sister that he had never had, and the thought of courting her had seemed out of the question at the time.

But she was back in Caldwell and as lovely as a woman could get. The age difference hadn't changed but somehow the implausibility of such a love affair developing had all but vanished, and so he knew he was going to have to watch himself very carefully where Miss Ruth Matheson was concerned.

Jim hadn't realized that Julia would be at Ruth's party, but here she was, larger than life and twice as stunning. The blue dress she had chosen to wear offset her stunning turquoise eyes perfectly, and she was rivalled by no woman present, except for Miss Ruth Matheson.

Jim keenly felt the awkwardness of it all. It had been a week since either he had been to see Julia at the mercantile or she had made the effort to see him at the sheriff's office, and he suspected she was still sore at him over the words they had exchanged. He wasn't sure whether she was going to be pleased to see him or not.

Making his way over to the drinks table, he poured himself a glass of punch and then leaning up against the wall in the corner of the room, cradled it in his hands and watched Julia as she worked her way around the room. It would only be a matter of time before she spotted him, and then he would have a better idea as to whether she had forgiven him for speaking his mind or not.

She was radiant, lighting up the room with her presence, working it like she was born to be the centre of attention, the eyes of every man in the room whether young or old were on her. Julia Brooks was in an elite class, and until just the other day she was the only woman in Caldwell that was in that class. But now she must share it with another, and as that rival entered the room the eyes that had until now been reserved for Julia were stolen away to focus on Ruth Matheson.

Jim's heart nearly stopped beating right then and there. He couldn't say the pale pink dress she had chosen to wear offset her eyes the same that Julia's dress offset hers, but that was because Ruth's vividly green ones completely eclipsed her competitors, so that no dress would do them justice as they flashed magically in the light of the room, mesmerizing every male who without exception found himself irresistibly drawn to them.

Julia noticed the attention being withdrawn from her, too, and as she turned around to look at her hostess managed a wan smile in Ruth's direction that did nothing to win back the admiring looks that had only moments ago been reserved for her.

Ruth's head was bobbing up and down and swinging ever so slightly from side to side as she navigated the crowded room looking for someone, and when she saw him up against that wall her face broke out into a delighted smile, a smile that Julia tracked all the way across the room to Jim Sandford.

'I'm glad you came,' Ruth said when she had evaded her numerous admirers and finally made it to where he was still clutching his untouched glass of punch.

'I couldn't pass up that dance you promised me.'

'As I seem to remember it was me who wheedled the promise out of you.'

He smiled warmly at her, 'You didn't need to wheedle very hard.'

Julia was suddenly there. Standing right beside Jim, she gave Ruth a frosty look before turning her attention to him. 'You haven't been to see me this week.'

Ruth looked from Jim to Julia and then back to Jim again, the smile she had given him as she walked over rapidly fading from her face. It was obvious she hadn't known of Jim's relationship with the Brooks woman.

'Now isn't the time to be discussing this, Julia,' Jim

71

said quietly, hoping she would display the decorum called for in the circumstances.

'Just when will be a good time, Jim?' Julia demanded, her hands now resting on her shapely hips in agitation. 'If we don't discuss it now when I've actually got your attention then you'll just let this whole business drag on.'

'Would you like me to leave the pair of you to talk?' Ruth asked meekly.

'Yes, I think that would be a good idea,' Julia responded with an air of authority. 'If I let him escape without having discussed it then I don't know when we'll get to clear this whole thing up.'

Ruth began to move off but Jim gently grabbed her by the wrist to stop her. 'Don't go, Ruth,' he said softly, 'we had only just started talking.'

Julia looked at him with fury in her blue eyes. 'Jim Sandford, I'm not used to being ignored like this. It has to stop. Do you understand?'

'I understand you are starting to make a spectacle of yourself, Julia. It would be best if you spent your time socializing. This is after all a party. I will stop off at the mercantile on Monday morning to talk about this if you wish.'

'It appears you are leaving me with no other choice.' Raising her head so her chin jutted out at him in defiance, she made eye contact for a moment before turning and sweeping off back into the crowded room.

'Oh dear, have I caused trouble between the two of you?'

'No, Julia is angry with me because we had words the other day. I get the impression she expected me to come to her with an apology this past week but I haven't because I don't believe I owe her one.'

'So it is a battle of the wills?'

'Something like that. My father always used to say that a man should start a relationship off in the way he intends it to continue. So because I don't want Julia to dictate everything to me I'm going to let her see I'm no pushover.'

Ruth's face dropped. 'So you and Julia are courting?'

'In a way I suppose we are.'

'In a way? That has to be the strangest answer to that question anyone has ever given me.'

'It's complicated, Ruth.'

'What is complicated about saying, "Yes I am courting that woman"?'

'We have seen each other a few times.'

'She seems to think it's more than that. I couldn't help but notice she wasn't happy about me talking to you.'

'I am beginning to think that Miss Julia Brooks is unhappy about a great number of things, Ruth, you talking to me being just one of them.'

The music started up then, a lively tune played by a very accomplished fiddler. 'I believe that is our cue,' Jim said, taking her by the hand and guiding her out onto the dance floor.

CHAPTER NINE

'I think you'd better get down to Brooks' Mercantile, Jim,' Bart said the moment he walked through the door of the sheriff's office.

Jim looked up from the newspaper he had been reading. 'Why's that?'

'There's big trouble brewing. I tried to quieten things down but neither man would listen.'

'Neither man . . . ?'

'Ethan Drake and Jake Westlake.'

Jim Sandford groaned. 'I had hoped that business was settled.'

'Ethan might have his water but Jake ain't happy about it.'

Jim's chair scraped noisily across the wooden floor as he got to his feet. 'Well this time I may have to bang heads together to get my point across.'

Bart Newcomb matched his boss stride for stride as they made their way down to the mercantile. Jim wasn't quite sure how he was going to handle the situation yet but he knew he had to nip this in the bud before it got completely out of hand. He had heard of arguments over water leading to fights, leading on to bloodshed, and there was no way he wanted that to happen in the sleepy little township of Caldwell.

The bell on the door over the shop rang loudly as they stepped inside, but Jim doubted anyone would have heard it above the raised voices coming from just in front of the counter.

'I've got as much right to that water as you have, Jake Westlake,' Ethan Drake's strained voice protested.

'Only because Jim Sandford says you have,' Westlake countered angrily. 'If he hadn't stuck his nose in and started throwing his weight around then you wouldn't be getting a single drop of it. It's a waste going to that rundown little holding you laughingly call a farm.'

'I make a living on that piece of dirt, I'll have you know.'

'If that's making a living I'd hate to see what you consider to be poverty, Drake.'

'You've just become too big for your boots because. . . .'

'All right, that's enough!' Jim hollered above the two arguing men.

Ethan Drake and Jake Westlake along with another dozen or so onlookers turned to see who it was who had snuck in unobserved and issued the loud demand.

'Well if it isn't the man himself,' Westlake said with disgust.

'Don't you speak ill of Jim Sandford,' Drake warned, 'he's the only man in Caldwell who cares about justice.'

'Or what ... what will you do?' Westlake moved forward and placing his hand on Ethan Drake's chest shoved him backwards.

'I ain't afraid to fight you, Jake Westlake,' Ethan said bravely as he regained his footing and stood toe to toe with the much bigger man.

'You will be after I've finished with you.'

'I said that's enough!' Jim roared with gusto. 'There'll be no fighting in this store, or anywhere else in Caldwell for that matter.'

It was as if Jake Westlake hadn't heard. Or maybe he had but just didn't care, for he picked the small man up with one hand until his feet left the floor and began to march him over to the door.

'You put me down, Jake Westlake,' Ethan insisted, his legs flailing wildly as he struggled to break free.

Westlake continued his journey towards the door of the mercantile.

'You heard him, Jake, put him down!' Jim was hard on the rancher's heels.

Westlake completely ignored him.

'I won't tell you again. Put Ethan down!'

Jake Westlake was on a mission, and that mission was to drop Ethan Drake on his backside in the dust of Caldwell's main street.

Slipping his Colt free of its holster Jim bellowed out once more. 'Last warning, Jake, put Ethan down.'

Jim Sandford brought the butt of the Colt down on the back of Jake Westlake's head the moment the cattleman's hand closed on the doorknob. With a grunt he dropped his victim, and then without any further ado crashed unceremoniously to the floor and lay there without so much as twitching.

'You've killed him,' a woman screamed.

Jim bent down and checked him over. 'He's all right,' he said as he straightened up again. 'If he had just done as he was told then I wouldn't have had to do that to him.'

'You're a brute,' the woman yelled. 'It's him you should have hit.' She pointed a trembling finger in Ethan Drake's direction. 'Nobody likes that horrible little man anyway.'

'It might pay for you to head off home now, Ethan,' Jim said quietly to him, sensing the mood of those present was about to turn ugly towards the crop farmer.

Disappointment was written all over Ethan Drake's face. He had done nothing wrong and yet he was being treated as the instigator of all the trouble. He had been minding his own business when he walked into the mercantile to buy a pound of nails for the new chicken coop he was building. It was Jake Westlake who had come in while he was at the counter paying for them and started the ruckus. Ranting about how he was going to lose money because Jim Sandford had ordered him to release his stored up water so Ethan could water his crops. The man was beside himself with fury and had been spoiling for a fight. As far as

Ethan was concerned he deserved to be hit over the head with Jim's Peacemaker.

Despite the unfairness of it Ethan did as suggested, and turning his back on everyone in the store he walked with head down out the door to leave them and the sorry township of Caldwell behind.

Jim turned to his deputy, 'Bart, could you organize a couple of fellers to help you carry Jake Westlake over to the sheriff's office, I reckon we're gunna have to charge him with disturbing the peace and maybe assault, too. He'll have to spend a day or so in one of the cells.'

Bart Newcomb nodded and set about dragging Jake Westlake's considerable bulk through the door with the help of one of Caldwell's citizens.

One by one the customers of Brooks' Mercantile paid for their purchases and filed away, no doubt eager to tell family and friends of the altercation they had just witnessed. Soon it would be all over town, and Jim assumed it would be Ethan Drake who would be painted the villain in it all. He hoped there wouldn't be a backlash against the man and his family, but somehow he suspected there would be.

'So are we going to discuss our relationship now?' Julia asked when everyone had gone and only she and Jim were left in the store.

'Now is as good a time as any I suppose.' He moved over to the counter to be closer to her.

'When we had that disagreement the other day I didn't think you would then avoid me for the rest of the week.'

78

'You could have come down to the sheriff's office to see me if you had a mind to,' he pointed out.

'The mood with which you left me that day made me wonder whether you would be happy to see me or not.'

'I seem to recall you saying you didn't want to speak to me and so I had no choice but to leave things at that.'

'Did I? I must confess I don't recall exactly what I did say to you, only that I was very upset.'

'As was I.'

'Could we forget all about it and start again do you think?'

'That is what I would prefer.'

Her face softened. 'I have been fretting about this all week. I'm glad it is out of the way now.'

Jim's thoughts were already elsewhere. 'What just took place here between Ethan and Jake has the potential to get completely out of hand. I don't want to see the Drake family vilified over this business.'

'I must confess I thought Jake Westlake overstepped the mark this time. Mr Drake was merely in here to buy some goods and not for an argument.'

'I'm afraid Jake Westlake, as likeable as he normally is, happens to have a vindictive streak that none of us were aware of until now. That's why I'm a little concerned for the Drakes.'

Julia looked alarmed. 'Do you think Jake will try to harm Mr Drake's family?'

'Not physically. But I think he's got it in him to do all he can to turn the folks of this town against them.

It would be easy enough for a man of Jake's standing to encourage those who think highly of him to ostracize the Drakes.'

'I hope he won't stoop that low, and I hope the rest of Caldwell doesn't either.'

Jim was pretty sure Jake Westlake was going to stoop that low, and when he did the rest of Caldwell would follow his example like the dumb sheep they reminded Jim of, but he didn't tell Julia that. Anything that might flare up another argument was strictly off limits for the time being, he had no desire to make up with her only to immediately find himself in her bad books again.

'Jim ... I need to know what is going on between you and the Matheson girl.' She had said it hesitantly, as if she feared the answer wouldn't be what she wanted to hear.

'Absolutely nothing,' he said honestly. 'Ruth and I are old friends who haven't seen each other in a couple of years.'

'I couldn't help noticing you danced with her rather a lot the other night. It seemed to me as if she only had eyes for you.'

'Did it? I know she used to be smitten with me when she was a girl. But that was a long time ago.'

'I think you may have to be careful there. It was obvious to everyone that she still holds a candle for you.'

'Does she? Well, I'll be on my guard from here on in then.'

He noticed Julia seemed satisfied with his answer.

Ruth Matheson posed a threat to any woman who wanted to keep a tight rein on her man. She was just so beautiful that it would take an exceptional man not to get carried away in her presence, and therefore risk making a fool not only of himself but also the woman he was supposed to be with.

She flashed him one of her special smiles. The kind she reserved for those who had pleased her. 'Will you come for dinner this Saturday?'

'I would like that, Julia. Maybe afterwards we could go for a ride in the gig if the weather is pleasant.'

'That would be very nice. I will see you on Saturday then.'

Jim left the mercantile with a weight lifted off his shoulders. He couldn't deny that he had been partly to blame for the argument that had developed between them the other day, even though he had found her attitude towards the poorer members of the community to be sorely lacking in compassion, but he would have been sad if their relationship had come to an end because of it, particularly given the fact that he had waited so many years to be given the chance of becoming Miss Julia Brooks' beau.

CHAPTER TEN

'There's a lot of talk in town that maybe electing you for sheriff was a mistake,' Bart said the next morning as he poured two cups of coffee from the old pot on the woodstove at the sheriff's office and handed one to Jim.

'On account of that business between Jake Westlake and Ethan Drake yesterday?'

'Yep, some folks are saying you ain't doin' the job they elected you for.'

'Me not bending the law to accommodate their friends is what irks them.'

'Maybe so, but there's talk of getting a petition together to call for your resignation.'

'If they can get enough signatures together then maybe I'll give them what they want.'

'Don't you dare, that'd leave me in charge and I don't fancy that, especially with the threat of Wade Baxter looming large.'

Jim had all but forgotten about Baxter amidst all the drama of the past week. But the mention of the outlaw's name brought his imminent arrival in Caldwell well and truly back to the top of his list of worries.

'He can't be too far away now,' Bart said, and then shot Jim a quick glance to see what his reaction to the statement was.

Jim smiled grimly. 'Taking on this job seemed like a good idea at the time but what with all that's been happening and now Wade Baxter to contend with I'm beginning to doubt the wisdom of that decision.'

'Being a sheriff of a small town like Caldwell is a thankless task at best, Jim.'

'I'm finding that out real fast. I couldn't get away from all the smiles and handshakes when I won the election, and now, only a few short weeks later almost no one wants to know me, and my only crime is I want to do everything by the book so it's all legal and right.'

'Folks don't want legal and right. They want what suits them best, and oftentimes that bears little resemblance to true justice.'

People could be hypocrites, Jim knew that only too well. They wanted justice when their rights were being impinged but it was a completely different matter when the boot was on the other foot. The rights of the little man like Ethan Drake didn't carry too much weight in the minds of most of the good folks of Caldwell, and that made Jim's job so much harder than it should be.

Bart jerked his thumb in the direction of the cells. 'What are we gunna do with that feller back there?'

'Charge him with disturbing the peace and fine him. Ethan Drake doesn't want to press assault charges against him so I guess we can let him go. Hopefully he won't stir things up against the Drakes as soon as he's free.'

'He's none too happy about the goose egg you gave him on the back of his head.'

'And I was none too happy having to give it to him. But he wouldn't leave Ethan be when I told him to so he paid the price.'

'There's talk amongst the businesses about barring the Drakes from buying from the stores in Caldwell.'

Jim frowned. 'That's just plain nasty. That feller has been through enough already without them making life impossible for him and his family.'

'I think the general sentiment is that if they refuse to sell anything to him he'll be forced to pack up and leave for greener pastures, Westlake will get all the water his heart desires, and everything will be back to the way they want it.'

'What crime has he committed for them to despise him so much?'

'He's different, Jim, and it doesn't pay to be different when you ain't rich. That's the only time you can get away with it.'

'It just ain't right what they're doing to him, Bart, and it makes me ashamed to say I'm a citizen of this town.' Jim was getting to see people he had known all his life in a very different light now he had a tin star pinned to his shirt. Maybe it was because he was dealing with them in the line of duty rather than just as a friend and neighbour that he was getting to see them warts and all. Sam Carrington must have been a saint to have put up with their pettiness for fifteen long years. Now Jim was beginning to see why the old man was so bitter towards them. He had ridden the storms created by their prejudice and small-minded-ness all that time and his reward for it all was their vote of no confidence in him. It would be enough to make any man bitter.

'You'll be a whole lot more ashamed than you are now by the time your tenure as sheriff is over. Being a sheriff means you get to see the very best in people but the very worst at times as well. Unfortunately it's the very worst that sticks in your mind for the longest and causes you so much grief.'

Jim stared at the door that led to the cells for a moment. 'Fine him and let him go. He's got a ranch to run and he can't do that from in here.'

Bart was gone for fifteen minutes before he walked back through with Jake Westlake. Pulling a six-gun and holster from the top drawer of the desk, he handed them to the rancher without saying a word.

As he strapped the gun-belt back on, Jake eyed Jim with undisguised contempt. 'You ain't the man I always took you to be,' he said when he had finished the task. 'In fact, you ain't half the man I took you to be.'

'I'm sorry you feel that way, Jake,' Jim said, taking the insult in his stride.

'You ain't gunna last long as sheriff of Caldwell, I can promise you that. You ain't gunna last long at all.'

'Maybe not. But at least I will be able to sleep at night knowing my integrity's intact, which is a whole heap more than you can say about yourself.'

If ever a man's eyes radiated pure hatred then Jake Westlake's did at that very moment. Jim wondered what would happen if they met on some dark road out of town one night with nobody around. Would that hatred escalate to violence? Jim wouldn't have thought it of the man a few days ago, but after his altercation with Ethan Drake he was no longer so sure.

'You can forget about me helping you out when Wade Baxter hits Caldwell. You can take him on without any of the men from the Double J standing by you.'

'That's fine by me, Jake. I would be nervous about whose back you'd be aiming your six-gun at anyway.' He knew the comment was a tad over the top but he was fed up with Jake Westlake's attitude. It was time he got back as good as he gave and who better to do that than Caldwell's new sheriff.

'You stinking, mangy, dog,' Westlake spat furiously, making a move towards Jim but stopping in his tracks when he saw the sheriff's hand go down and rest on the butt of his six-gun. 'You've already used that thing on me once so I don't doubt you'd use it again,' he said sourly.

'You'd better believe I would. I've got no time for

a man who behaves as badly as you do. You might be the biggest rancher around these parts but that doesn't put you above the law. Yep, I'll use my gun on any man who oversteps the mark.' He jerked his head in the direction of the door. 'Now get out before I throw you out, and if you do anything to cause me to lock you up again, be warned that I'll make sure your stay is for much longer than this one has been.'

Westlake's fury was visible, but he managed to contain his desire to smash his fist into the side of the upstart sheriff's head. Wade Baxter would deal with Jim Sandford, and Westlake for one would be there to clap his hands in joy at the sight of Sandford lying in a pool of his own blood out there in the main street of Caldwell. Without saying another word, he strode angrily from the sheriff's office to get his horse from the livery stables and head back to the ranch.

'Forget about him giving Ethan Drake trouble,' Bart said as he watched the man stalk up the street from his position by the window, 'it's more the trouble he might give you that you should be worrying about.'

'Jake Westlake is the least of my worries at the moment. It's Wade Baxter who has the potential to tear this town apart, and without Jake Westlake on our side things have just got a whole heap harder.' Jim had been displaying a certain amount of bravado when he had told Jake he would be nervous about whose back he would be pointing his pistol at, but the truth was, he had needed the man's help and now that it was withdrawn from him he was no longer so confident he would handle the arrival of Wade Baxter too well. There were still men in Caldwell he and Bart could call on when the shooting started, but they wouldn't be as capable as Jake Westlake and his men would have been.

'I can ask around town and see who's prepared to make a stand with us if you like,' Bart offered.

Jim nodded. 'That might be a good idea. Talk to John Anderson down at the gunsmith shop. He told me he'd stand by me if I ever needed him to. But after all that's happened in recent days he may have changed his mind.'

'I'll pop in and see him this morning before I ask some of the other fellers I'm thinking would stand by us. It certainly wouldn't hurt to know who is gunna be available before Baxter evens gets here.'

Jim was getting increasingly anxious on that score. If folks started siding with Jake Westlake then come the time Baxter drifted into Caldwell there may well only be a handful of men prepared to strap on a gun and lend Jim a hand. The problem was, Jim had no idea how many men Wade Baxter would be bringing with him when he did get here. It may be only one or two, or it may be considerably more.

'How about you get on to that right away?' Jim suggested. 'I don't think we can set our minds at rest until we're sure.'

'Right,' Bart flipped his Stetson off the peg beside the door and planted it firmly on top of his mop of unruly brown hair, 'I'll be back with the verdict in a couple of hours.'

Jim smiled to himself as Deputy Bart Newcomb stepped out the door and disappeared from sight. He didn't know what he would do if he didn't have the loyal and capable fellow watching his back. He would be a great support when push came to shove, and Jim couldn't think of anyone in Caldwell he would prefer to have at his side more than Bart Newcomb.

Jim wondered just how Baxter was going to play this out. Would he try to take down one man at a time starting with the one he figured harmed him the most? Or would he just ride into town with all guns blazing and kill all and sundry that stood in his way? There was no telling with a man like Wade Baxter. More than twenty years busting rocks in a quarry while hating those who had put him there could do things to a man that would make him unpredictable, volatile even. A man like that driven by the lust for revenge could be capable of doing just about anything Jim figured, so he would have to expect the unexpected and be ready for all contingencies.

Bart returned a couple of hours later and, slinging his Stetson back on the peg beside the door, moved over to the coffee pot on the stove to pour himself a brew.

Jim shoved the wanted posters he had been looking at back in the top drawer of the desk and gave him his full attention. 'Good news or bad?'

'Anderson's still with you, as are several other men in town. I figure we can still put up a united front when Baxter gets here.'

'What about Harrison Brooks?'

Bart shook his head. 'He told me to tell you that he won't risk his store getting burned down or shot up on account of Wade Baxter. He reckons he's just a storekeeper and that it's you who's been hired to take care of rabble rousers like Baxter.'

'I'm surprised at his attitude. I would have thought he would have wanted Baxter stopped in his tracks before he causes too much mayhem. He must know you and I can't handle this thing on our own.'

Bart shrugged his bony shoulders. 'A man like Harrison has a lot to lose I suppose. It took him years to get the money together to build that mercantile and stock it. Years more to get it to make the kind of profit it's making for him now. He doesn't want to risk losing it all.'

'That's exactly what will happen if Wade Baxter has his way. Harrison was one of those men who helped put him away all those years ago. I doubt Baxter has forgotten that.'

'Nope, I reckon you're right there. I wouldn't have forgotten if it was me either. But Harrison is trying to keep his head down and away from all the action in the hope that he might come through this unscathed. Now that sounds foolish to you and me, but at his age he isn't really up to exchanging lead with much younger men, and if he was foolish enough to try then the chances are pretty good that he'll be the one stopping most of that lead.'

What Bart had just said made sense. But Jim was still disappointed in the older man not being prepared to help out in some way or other. He had a lot to gain by Jim coming up trumps in this conflict, and so surely that demanded something in the way of support.

CHAPTER ELEVEN

Jim strapped on the left-handed holster he had just bought from John Anderson and attempted a quick draw. The Peacemaker cleared leather fast but his finger never found the trigger, nor did his palm close tightly on the grips, and so instead of the pistol coming to life in his hand like he needed it to, it merely clattered noisily onto the floor of the sheriff's office.

'Dang it,' Jim muttered angrily to himself as he stooped down to pick it up. He wasn't going to present much of a threat to Wade Baxter like this. Sitting down, he carefully unwrapped the bandages from his injured gun hand and inspected the damage.

It was still swollen even a week after Kurt Butler had walloped it with that wooden club. The doc had warned him it would take a long time to heal, but for some reason Jim had decided to suspend reality for the fantasy that it would be back to normal before Wade Baxter arrived in Caldwell. Well, he had just had a mighty big reality check. That hand was weeks away from being able to do anything at all.

So, the left hand it was then. He would have to practise long and hard every day until he was pulling iron just as fast with his left hand as he ever did with his right. He just hoped he was a fast learner, because he doubted Wade Baxter was much more than six days away from reaching town now, and with the sheriff of Caldwell fronting up to the outlaw with a useless gun hand all he would achieve would be the man's contempt.

The imminent arrival of Wade Baxter had completely dominated his thoughts these past few days. This would be the biggest test he had ever faced either as sheriff or during his years as deputy, and he figured it may be the biggest test he would ever face. Dang it, maybe it would be the last he would face if he didn't learn to pull iron like a professional gunman over the next few days.

Julia walked into the sheriff's office just then and broke him free of his thoughts. 'I brought you something to eat because I doubt you've been looking after yourself,' she said, and then with a smile laid a freshly baked apple pie down on the desk in front of him.

'You must have read my mind. I swear I was just about to head on down to the café to see what they could rustle up for me.'

'No need to now.' She handed him a fork.

Digging it in Jim lifted a piece to his mouth and sampled it. Not bad, he decided. In fact, it was better than not bad. If the rest of Julia's cooking was like this then he could happily settle down with her safe in the knowledge he wouldn't be condemning himself to a lifetime of culinary disasters.

'Jim, I need to tell you something that I know you're not going to like,' she said suddenly, and not without a certain amount of trepidation.

Here we go, Jim thought, as he placed the fork down. 'Go ahead,' he said quietly.

'Pa has banned the Drake family from purchasing anything from Brooks' Mercantile. Jake Westlake came in this morning and he and Pa had a little talk and Jake persuaded Pa to see things his way.'

'Jake threatened not to buy anything from the store if Harrison didn't ban the Drakes, I suppose,' Jim said, realizing the type of persuasion she meant.

Staring at a spot on the floor, Julia nodded.

Jake Westlake had Harrison Brooks over a barrel. He was the one man in Caldwell who had the power to make or break a business. The purchasing power of his ranch was such that nearly every business in Caldwell relied on it to remain profitable, if Westlake withdrew his custom than it spelt financial ruin for that business.

'The more I get to know that man the less I like him,' Jim admitted.

'Pa doesn't think too highly of him any more either,' Julia confessed. 'He walked into our mercantile like he owned the place, and when Pa said he wouldn't bar anyone from buying goods from us Mr Westlake flew into a rage and said if he didn't bar the

Drake family he would see Pa destitute. Pa had no choice but to go along with it then.'

'We always have a choice, Julia. It's just that sometimes that choice will have serious repercussions for us.'

'I hope you aren't suggesting that Pa has behaved in a cowardly manner.'

'That's not for me to say. You father must make his decisions based on what his conscience tells him to do not mine.'

'But you wouldn't have given in to Mr Westlake?'

'No, I wouldn't have given in to him.'

'Even knowing that it might cost you everything you've worked your entire life for?'

'Even then.'

'That sounds very naïve to me, Jim.'

'A man has to have a code to live his life by, Julia, or he'll be bent every which way by just about everyone. There are some things I just wouldn't do, and ostracizing someone to the point of starving them off their land is most definitely one of them.'

'I still don't think Pa had any choice.'

'And it's your right to believe that if you choose to.'

'Now you are making it sound as if I'm the one who is being unreasonable.'

Jim sighed. There was no way he was going to win this one and so the best policy was to quit before things got too heated. 'I would never say that of you,' he said diplomatically.

'But you would think it?'

'Julia, I don't want to fall out with you again.'

He could see she was annoyed with him even though she didn't answer. To her mind there was nothing more important than financial survival and all other considerations took a back seat to that. To Jim there was nothing more important than seeing justice was done, nothing should supersede that.

'I thought you would want to know what Mr. Westlake is up to,' she said icily. 'I will leave you to get on with your paperwork now.'

'Thank you, Julia,' Jim said in as conciliatory tone as he could. 'And please tell your father that I am sorry he is being placed in such a difficult position.'

She nodded and then without saying another word crossed the floor to the door and was gone.

Jim was acutely aware that this feud between the Westlakes and the Drakes had placed him and Julia on opposite sides. How they were going to get through the bitterness and animosity that was bound to become a part of everyday life in Caldwell from here on in he did not know, he only knew that she had long been the girl of his dreams and he desperately wanted things to work out between them, and if they didn't then he was going to be one mighty disappointed man.

Pouring himself a coffee, he took it over to his desk and, settling into his chair, tried to come up with a solution to Ethan Drake's problem. Unable to buy much of anything in Caldwell anymore, he wasn't going to last the winter out on that little farm of his. He relied on selling the bulk of his produce, and if no one in town was going to buy it then it would only be a matter of time before his existence on that smallholding became untenable. Jim might be able to buy what Ethan needed and quietly get it out to him without anybody being any the wiser, but he couldn't do anything about selling Ethan's produce for him.

Sipping the hot black liquid, Jim stared out the window at the goings on in the street outside and felt bad for the man and his family. The poor long-suffering wife who worked from first light until well after the sun went down to cook, clean, milk the house cow, tend that big vegetable garden, raise the children, and work in the fields alongside her husband when necessity demanded it, was going to lose what little she and her husband had broken their backs for because of the greed of just one man who wasn't satisfied with the abundance he already had.

Jim had stood for sheriff to make a difference to the lives of people like the Drakes. But oh how he felt keenly that he was letting them down. There must be some way he could turn this around, but try as he might he just couldn't come up with a solution.

The opinions of a man like Jake Westlake could race through the population of a town like Caldwell just as thoroughly as yeast through a tub of dough. First, those who were well-to-do would side with the man because they too understood the lust for more money that was achieved by expanding one's business empire. They in turn would bring pressure to bear on those struggling businesses to join them in their condemnation of the man who stood in the way of *progress* until there wouldn't be a man or woman in town brave enough to stand up for the little man's rights, for fear of the backlash against themselves should they be foolish enough to do so.

Yes, so called *civilized* man had a long way to go yet, and the only thing standing in the way of the poor and downtrodden being swept completely away was the laws this great nation had enacted to protect them, such as the water right that said Ethan Drake was granted the licence to draw what he needed to water his crops and livestock and that no one could prevent him from doing so. It was up to men like Jim to make sure that licence wasn't violated, and if that was going to make him unpopular with the citizens of Caldwell then they had no one to blame but themselves. After all, they were the ones who had elected him sheriff.

CHAPTER TWELVE

Jim heard them long before he saw them. When they finally did come into sight they were riding hell for leather past the smithy at the end of the street, dust billowing up in a thick cloud as high as the bellies of the sweating, heavily breathing mounts they were riding.

Jim abandoned his perusal of the rump steak in the butcher's shop window; all thoughts of his supper discarded at this latest development, and gave his full attention to the six riders as they pulled up abruptly outside the Lonely Bull Saloon. They looked like trouble, with their low-slung guns, and when they dismounted and swaggered self-confidently into the bar to wash the dust from their throats he knew it wouldn't be long before there would be complaints concerning them.

He got to thinking where they might have come from, and it was then that his heart leapt into his throat. Of course, they could be none other than Wade Baxter and his men, he hadn't been expecting them for another five or six days so the fact it could be them hadn't entered his head right away. But it would be them sure enough, they were no ordinary cowpokes. All six wore their shooting irons in the manner of gunfighters.

The door of the butcher shop opened and as Jeb Thompson stepped out wiping his bloody hands on his apron he peered anxiously up the street. 'Did you just see that, Sheriff?'

'A little hard for me to miss I reckon, Mr Thompson,' he said to the older man.

'Any idea who they might be?'

'Wade Baxter and his men would be my guess.'

The man shook his head. 'Wade Baxter wasn't amongst them.'

Jim's eyes left the front door of the saloon and travelled to Thompson's, 'You sure?'

'Just as sure as I can see you standing here. I knew Wade Baxter better'n anyone when he made Caldwell his home twenty odd years ago, and none of those hombres looked anything like him. Besides, those fellers were all too young to be Baxter. There wasn't a man over thirty amongst them, and Baxter'd be going on forty-six now I reckon.'

Jim thought about what he had just been told. If Baxter wasn't one of them then just who in blazes were they? There could be no doubt they were all gunfighters, that much was obvious, but why would they be in Caldwell if they had nothing to do with Wade Baxter? Could it be he had sent them on ahead to scout out the lay of the land? Was it their brief to report to him whether they thought the law in Caldwell might give him trouble if he attempted to put his plan of retribution into practice?

That had to be it. There could be no other explanation. Six gunfighters and Wade Baxter himself, that was going to be a tall order for Jim, Bart, and a handful of the local men to tame. It would have been a cinch with Jake Westlake and the men of the Double J Ranch at his back, but not now, not with only five or six men willing to make a stand with him, and none of them except Bart being any good with a gun. This whole business had just taken a turn for the worse, Wade Baxter had the upper hand, and being the law in Caldwell, Jim knew he was in it up to his neck.

'Whoever they are they looked like trouble to me,' Thompson said matter-of-factly. 'I'm pleased it ain't me who has to make them toe the line. It's times like this I'm glad I'm a butcher.' He smiled grimly at Jim. 'If you do have to go down there and sort them out then make sure you don't go alone. Take some good men with you. I wouldn't like your chances of coming out alive if you don't.'

'And are you volunteering to be one of the men I take with me, Mr Thompson?'

The fellow gave an involuntary shudder. 'No fear. I'm not stupid enough to go up against seasoned gunfighters, and that's what they all are, I reckon. Nope, I'll leave that to them who wear the badge, after all, that's what we pay you fellers for.'

Jim watched the retreating back of Caldwell's sole

butcher as he abandoned the boardwalk for the relative safety of his shop and wondered how many more of the townsmen would share his opinion. It was probably that same attitude that had allowed Baxter to run riot in Caldwell the last time he had been here, and if they were all too self-serving to break free of that attitude then it would allow the outlaw to do it again.

With a heavy heart, Jim stepped down off the boardwalk and trudged wearily across the street to the sheriff's office to break the bad news to Bart.

'Dang, that's not what I wanted to hear,' the deputy said after Jim had told him each and every man had carried his weapon in the style of a professional gunman. 'That'll make it harder to get anyone to stand by us when the shooting starts.'

That possibility hadn't been lost on Jim either. He knew from experience that the ordinary cowpuncher, storekeeper, bartender, or what have you, would lend a hand if he was sure there wasn't much chance he could lose his life. There was safety in numbers, seemed to be the reasoning. But if he found out he would be pitted against a man who made his living by hiring out his gun then you wouldn't see him for the dust. This was beginning to look like it might be one of those times.

'We're gunna need some help, Jim, and I don't mean the usual run of the mill sort either. We need at least two men who can handle a gun along with the best of them.'

Jim sighed. 'I know, Bart, but where do we get them? Caldwell doesn't boast anyone who can trade lead with a gunfighter.'

'Except you and me and you've got a busted up gun hand.'

Jim stared at the bandaged hand for a moment. 'I'm getting better with my left.'

'Good enough to out-draw one of Baxter's men?'

Jim shook his head. 'Not yet.'

'Then this is beginning to look like a no win situation for us.'

Jim knew it. 'But if we don't make a stand then Baxter's gunna pick off those he has a grudge against one by one until they're all dead.'

'And probably plenty who had nothing to do with his incarceration as well. Once he gets that blood lust under way there'll be no stopping him.'

Jim had heard of men like Wade Baxter before, men who had been put away for decades who hadn't been softened by the passage of time. The harsh treatment meted out to them in whatever penal institution they had been incarcerated had hardened them beyond all salvation, and when they finally gained their freedom they were no longer men in the true sense of the word, but rather, unfeeling, uncompromising killers who would think nothing of taking a human life if it suited their purposes. For them, going back to prison meant little compared to satisfying the vengeance that had kept them sane through long years of manual labour designed to break their spirit. Men like that would risk their newfound freedom and even their lives rather than forgo the pleasure that getting even brought to them.

'What are we gunna do about these six fellers down at the saloon?'

'There's nothing we can do until they've done something wrong,' Jim answered evenly.

'I reckon that won't be too far off. Get some hard liquor inside them and trouble will be a dead certainty rather than a mere possibility.'

Bart was right and Jim knew it. But he had to play this by the book, and as yet they hadn't done anything to warrant the law getting involved. But when they did, and Bart was right in saying they would, then Jim had better have a plan in place to counter them or all hell was going to break loose in the normally sleepy town of Caldwell.

Jim wondered how Sam Carrington would handle this if he was still sheriff. Would he have taken his three deputies with him down to the saloon and told those six gunmen to climb back on their horses and ride on out of Caldwell? Or would he have adopted a wait and see approach? Jim didn't know what the older man would have done in the early days of his career but he knew that in his final days he would have waited it out and hoped nothing came of it. That's what happened when a man grew too old and complacent for the job. But Jim didn't believe that option lay open to him. No, he would have to find out what these boys were up to, and he would have to do it now.

'Grab yourself a shotgun from the rack,' he said to Bart as he stood up and pushed his chair aside.

'Where we goin'?'

'To the saloon, to see what these hombres are about.'

'Is that wise?'

'Nope, but I ain't going to wait around here twiddling my thumbs and hoping they ain't gunna give us any trouble. It's time we found out what their intentions are.'

'And you reckon they're gunna tell you just like that?'

'If I ask them the right way they will.'

'And what way is that?'

'Come along and you'll find out.'

Selecting a light shotgun, Jim made sure it was loaded and then waited for Bart to do the same.

'I hope you ain't leading me to my death, Jim,' Bart said as he clicked the barrel shut and stuffed half a dozen cartridges into his shirt pocket.

'Neither of us needs to die if we play this right.'

'And how is that?'

'I need you to come in through the back door to the saloon while I come through the front. Keep yourself hidden behind the door until I need you. I reckon they'll tell me what I want to hear because they'll think I'm on my own and easy to take. As soon as I know what they're planning I'll get you to step into the barroom and show them your shotgun. With me in front of them and you behind I don't reckon they'll try anything.'

'You do know about the best laid plans of mice and men, don't you?'

Jim Sandford grinned at his deputy's comment. 'Let's hope they're gunna be mice when they see two fellers holding a couple of scatterguns on them.'

Jim gave Bart five minutes to get in place before he pushed the batwings apart and entered the smoky interior of the Lonely Bull Saloon. He allowed himself a moment or two to scout out the room and locate where the six men were sitting before he left the safety of the open doorway. He was halfway across the floor when one of the men spotted him and, saying something to the others, they turned in their chairs to watch Jim as he covered the rest of the floor to stand in front of them. 'Howdy, boys,' he said calmly. 'I noticed you ride into town twenty minutes back and decided to drop in and say hello.'

'Now ain't that mighty civil of you, Sheriff,' one of the men said. 'Ain't that civil of the tin star, boys?' He glanced around at his friends, a big grin on his face.

The other five men chuckled at the fellow's little joke.

'You boys planning on being in town long?'

'Well now, that kinda depends, Sheriff.'

Jim decided to play his game for a while, 'On what exactly?'

'On how much we happen to like the place.'

'We like the place just fine,' Jim said coolly, 'and that's the way we aim to keep it.'

'I can't think what you mean by that, Sheriff.'

'Oh I think you do.'

'Nope, but you could always spell it out for us.'

'I figure you boys are riding with Wade Baxter,' he watched the fellow's face carefully for any sign that might tell him he had it right, but he wasn't giving anything away. 'I also think he's sent you into Caldwell ahead of him so you can see if the law here is gunna give him any trouble when he arrives.'

'You've got it all worked out ain't you, tin star?'

'I reckon I have, little man.'

The gunman bristled at the insult. He was used to being the one dishing out the putdowns. But here was this no account sheriff waltzing in here on his lonesome and speaking down to him as if he had nothing to fear by doing so. He was soon going to be a dead sheriff if he carried on in this vein.

'You're one high and mighty feller,' Baxter's man said with venom. 'You ain't gunna last much longer in the job if you don't learn to remember your place.'

'If you or any of these barrel boarders sitting next to you try and give me any trouble I'll make sure you regret it,' Jim said in a deep menacing tone. 'And you can tell Wade Baxter he ain't welcome in Caldwell. He was run out once before and he'll be run out again if need be.'

A chair scraped across the whiskey-stained floor as the man got to his feet. 'You're a mighty big talker for a lawman on his own,' he said with a tinge of anger in his voice.

Jim grinned at him. 'Who said I was alone?'

Knowing the tricks of the trade, the gunfighter

glanced briefly over his shoulder, spotting Bart standing not more than seven or eight yards away. Both barrels of the shotgun he was holding were trained on those sitting at the table.

'You're slick, I'll give you that, tin star,' he said scornfully. 'But that's not gunna be enough to keep you alive when Wade gets here.'

So it was true, they were riding with Wade Baxter, Jim had thought as much. It wouldn't be long before Baxter joined them either. 'Your boss tries anything in Caldwell and this will become his permanent home. There's a plot in the cemetery up on the hill with his name on it.'

'That's mighty big talk coming from a sheriff with just one deputy to back him up.'

The grin hadn't left Jim's face for a second. 'What makes you think I've only got the one deputy?'

'I know plenty about you, Sheriff Jim Sandford.'

Someone in town had been talking. Maybe it was Jake Westlake, determined to get his own back on the upstart sheriff who had spoiled his plans. Whoever it was, Wade Baxter and his men now knew Jim was seriously understaffed when it came to law enforcement officers, and that would have been why they had ridden so openly and boldly into town.

Now it was the outlaw's turn to grin. 'You ain't so cocky now are you, tin star?'

Jim's eyes left the man and took in the countenance of each and every one of Baxter's men. They were all grinning at him as if he was well out of his depth and should know it. It was the confidence younger men often displayed when they thought they held the upper hand, even though they had no way of knowing whether they really did or not.

'Wade is coming to Caldwell whether you like it or not, and when he does there's gunna be a reckoning for those who did him wrong and those who try to stop him. So maybe you should just hand in your badge and ride on out of here while you still can. At the moment Wade doesn't have any beef with you.'

'Maybe what my deputy and I should do is empty both our barrels into you sorry excuses for men and be done with it,' Jim countered, and then took satisfaction in the fact he saw a slight look of fear in the fellow's eyes.

'Now you really are making an enemy out of Wade. He ain't gunna like it when I tell him about this.'

'Wade Baxter can go hang himself,' Jim said curtly. 'He's nothing more than a low-down dirty skunk who should have had a rope put around his neck years ago, and you can tell him that from me.'

'You really do have a death wish, tin star, and believe me, Wade will make sure that wish comes true.'

'Talk is cheap, little man. Now drop your gun-belt, and you other men can do the same as well.'

The man looked back at Jim with fury in his grey eyes. 'I don't drop my gun-belt for any man!'

'Then I have the authority as sheriff of this town to blow you clear across the room.' He gave it a moment for his threat to sink in. 'I'm gunna give you exactly five seconds to unbuckle it and if you don't then I'm gunna pull this trigger.'

If he thought he could have beaten Jim to it the fellow would have gone for his gun, but there was something about this particular man that told him this lawman was no ordinary sheriff, and if he wanted to carry on breathing he had better do as he was told. With the greatest of reluctance, he unstrapped his gun-belt and let it drop without any fanfare to the sawdust-covered floor of the Lonely Bull Saloon.

'You've just made the biggest mistake of your life, tin star,' he growled throatily.

'Plenty of fellers have told me that in the past, little man, but I'm still here and most of them are not.' He jerked his head in the direction of the batwings. 'Now, get out of Caldwell, and if you come back you better be prepared to trade some lead.'

All six gunmen sauntered slowly across the floor of the crowded saloon, desperately trying to salvage as much pride from their embarrassing situation as they possibly could. Covering them from the doorway with their shotguns, the two lawmen made sure they didn't reach for a rifle or saddle-bag pistol and try to regain entry to the saloon.

'Well that put the cat amongst the pigeons,' Bart said as the last of them disappeared beyond the smithy at the far end of town. 'We are now officially on the list of fellers Wade Baxter will be determined to send to Boot Hill.'

'I reckon we were already on that list, on account of the fact each of us wears a badge and Wade Baxter hates anyone or anything to do with the law.'

They were gone, but Jim was under no illusions as to whether they would be back, and when they did it would be with vengeance on their minds and a loaded gun in each of their hands.

CHAPTER THIRTEEN

Jim looked up to see who it was who had walked through the door of the sheriff's office and was surprised to discover it was Ruth Matheson. He had figured she would have kept a low profile where he was concerned now she knew he had been seeing Julia Brooks.

'I have something to tell you that I think you'll be interested to know,' she said in her soft feminine voice. She had a worried look on her face that told him what she was about to say was deeply troubling her.

With his coffee cup in one hand and a newspaper in the other he looked at her expectantly. If there was one thing he remembered about the girl it was that she never beat around the bush, she would need no prompting from him to say what was on her mind.

'I heard from Millie Jones there were six men in Caldwell yesterday. She said they were all gunmen. She had been told they are Wade Baxter's men.'

'That's right, they are.'

'I was out riding this morning and about an hour ago I stopped to rest the mare in a grove of cotton-wood trees. While I was there six men rode up and reined up their horses. They didn't see me as they didn't come into the grove, but I could see them well enough as they had the sun shining on them whereas I was in the shadows of the trees.'

'And. . . ?'

'A seventh man rode up and I could hear him talking to them about you and how he would tell them anything they needed to know about Caldwell and its citizens in exchange for them helping him to kill you.'

So it hadn't been Jake Westlake who had been in cahoots with Wade Baxter after all. Jim had seen him striding down the main street of Caldwell about an hour back as if he owned the entire town, there was no way he could have been in Caldwell and where Ruth had seen the informer at the same time. He felt relieved. If Westlake and the hands on the Double J Ranch had joined forces with Baxter then Jim and Bart wouldn't have stood a chance. 'Did you get a good look at this seventh man?' Jim asked hopefully.

She nodded her pretty head. 'It was Kurt Butler.'

He should have known. In the drama over water rights and Ethan Drake being banned from the stores in Caldwell, Jim had plum forgotten about that fellow. But he obviously hadn't forgotten how Jim had romanced Julia Brooks, the girl he considered to be his, and locked him up for attacking him. He had received a hefty fine for his crime, too. It stood to reason he would be the one feeding Baxter information in an attempt to bring about Jim's demise. He was just vicious enough to want to see Jim dead, too.

'Thank you for telling me, Ruth,' he said sincerely.

'Please be careful, Jim. These men aim to kill you and all you have to help you is Bart. The two of you can't stand up to Wade Baxter and his men on your own.'

'Now don't you go worrying yourself about that,' he said, putting his coffee cup and newspaper down and crossing the floor to stand next to her.

'But I do. You know how I feel about you. I've always loved you and I always will. I know you are in love with Julia Brooks and there can never be anything between us, but if something were to happen to you I would be devastated for the rest of my life.'

As tears formed in her eyes he wished he could put her mind at ease, but the reality was he was up against a formidable foe and was heavily outnumbered. There was a very good chance that something untoward would happen to him.

'I will do whatever I can to help you,' she continued, her voice trembling as she spoke. 'You only have to ask. I know how to handle a rifle, my pa taught me before I went to live with my aunt.'

He placed his big hand on her shoulder in a gesture of gratitude. 'Keep your eyes and ears open and report to me anything you hear,' he answered, more to make her feel she could be of help than anything else. The truth was he didn't want her to get mixed up in this business at all. If something happened to her on account of him he would never forgive himself.

She smiled through the tears. 'I'll do everything I can,' she promised.

'You'd best get yourself off,' he said, suddenly realizing how dangerous it was for her to be there. 'If Butler sees you coming in here he'll put two and two together and realize you mean something to me and tell Wade Baxter. Your life would be in serious danger then, and I can't allow for anything to happen to you.'

Her eyes widened as she looked at him in surprise. 'Do I mean something to you?'

'Of course you do. I have always been very fond of you, Ruth, surely you knew that.'

She managed a smile then, and the thought struck him that maybe she hadn't. Without any warning she went up on tiptoe and kissed him on the lips before scuttling out the door like a small child who had just done something she knew was very naughty.

After she had gone Jim thought how she had displayed more courage than most of the men in this town. If he gave her a gun and told her to stand next to him when Baxter and his men came thundering into Caldwell then he had no doubt she would do it. Sometimes when the chips were down valour came from the most unlikely quarter.

He would have to get Kurt Butler arrested on some charge and keep him locked up until this business with Wade Baxter was over. He couldn't have the man paving the way for the outlaw to wreak his intended havoc upon the citizens of Caldwell. Jim wasn't going to give Wade Baxter any advantage if it was within his power to prevent it. He would have to watch for an opportunity to lock Butler up. He didn't know what charge he could get him on yet but he was sure the man would slip up soon enough and then Jim would have all the excuse he needed to reacquaint the fellow with a prison cell.

His chance came later that afternoon as he was doing his rounds, keeping a wary eye out for Wade Baxter and his men, half expecting them to hurtle into town at any moment, with hoofs thumping out an ominous rhythm on the hard surface of the street, and their mounts' faces flecked with foam. But instead, as he wandered up a side street who should he spy but Kurt Butler himself perched precariously on the crumbling stone wall that enclosed the house and property of the old widow Martha Gresham, and he was reaching up into a tree about to pick a ripe juicy apple.

'I've got you now,' Jim said quietly to himself as he tucked himself out of sight and waited for the fellow to pluck the apple and sink his teeth into it.

Jumping down off the wall with apple in hand and a satisfied smirk on his face, Butler continued on down the street to where Jim suddenly stepped out from behind a tree and confronted him.

'Afternoon, Mr. Butler,' he said in a low no nonsense tone. 'I see you've now stooped to stealing your food instead of working for it.'

Butler looked at Jim then the apple and back at Jim again. 'This is my apple, Sandford,' he said aggressively.

'Then would you mind telling me where you got it from?'

'I brought it from home.'

'But you don't have any apple trees at your place.'

'I bought a bag of them at the greengrocers and took them home,' he said quickly, hoping to cover his tracks.

'So if we go down to the greengrocers and asked them if you'd bought some apples off them in the last few days they'd say yes?'

'Yep, they would.'

'You lying skunk, Butler. I just watched you standing on Widow Gresham's wall while you stole that apple from her tree.'

Kurt Butler returned Jim a sulky look. 'So what . . . it's just an apple.'

'It's stealing is what it is and that's against the law.'

'It's just an apple,' Butler said again but with an angrier countenance this time.

'Stealing is stealing, Butler, and so I'm afraid I'm going to have to arrest you for it.'

'You ain't gunna do nothing of the sort,' he retorted furiously.

'Aren't I? Well you just watch me. Hand over your sidearm!'

'You ain't arresting me for taking an apple,' Butler insisted.

117

'If I have to use my gun then I will,' Jim warned.

Butler dropped the apple and foolishly went for his gun but Jim was ready for him and had his new Colt out of its holster and pointed at him first. 'Drop it or I'll shoot!' he barked.

Realizing the futility of finishing his draw, Kurt Butler let the pistol drop from his hand.

'Now, start walking towards the sheriff's office. You've got a lengthy stay in one of the cells ahead of you.'

With Kurt Butler safely locked up Jim had not only shut down Wade Baxter's flow of information, but he had saved himself from getting shot in the back as well. Butler had proved he wasn't averse to a sneak attack, and so when Wade Baxter got to town and the bullets started flying there would have been nothing to stop Butler from positioning himself out of sight, then waiting for an opportune moment to pay the sheriff back and make it look like one of Baxter's men had done it. With him off the streets it was one fewer worry for Jim to trouble himself with. As far as Jim was concerned, Kurt Butler could stay locked up until the circuit judge was next in Caldwell, and that may very well be a couple of months away.

Baxter would be camped somewhere a few miles out of town waiting for an opportune time to ride into Caldwell and seek his revenge. His men would have told him there was only one deputy backing up the sheriff, but that the sheriff was one ornery cuss who wasn't to be taken lightly. Chances were, now that Baxter knew the type of man Jim Sandford was he would try to gun him down before he started on his rampage of retribution, rather than get on to the job first and deal to him if he tried to stand in his way.

Jim knew he was still up against it, and if he wanted to even up this contest he needed at least one more man who could handle a gun along with the best of them. If he could find such a man then there would be a glimmer of a chance that he could beat Wade Baxter at his own game. But where on earth would he come up with such a man at such short notice? Little was he to know that such a man was heading for Caldwell at this very moment, and he was a man who could strike fear into the heart of even a hardened criminal like Wade Rueben Baxter.

CHAPTER FOURTEEN

He sat tall in the saddle, his poise and unaffected air singling him out as a man who was not only sure of himself but whom also possessed a great deal of natural ability. As he rode casually past the café Jim was eating in, the sheriff of Caldwell could see through the well-polished window that the man was a gunfighter, and because he was on his own he doubted he was riding with Wade Baxter's bunch.

Jim watched him until he reined his appaloosa gelding up and, dismounting, disappeared into the Lonely Bull Saloon. Was this the fellow he needed to swing things back in his favour where Wade Baxter was concerned?

He waited for the stranger to come out of the saloon before getting up from his meal and walking out onto the boardwalk. Rolling himself a cigarette, he lit it before giving it pride of place in the corner of his mouth, the grey smoke curling lazily past the top of his head to disappear under the roof of the boardwalk.

The gunfighter walked slowly back up Caldwell's main thoroughfare as he led the appaloosa, his keen eye taking in every movement on both sides of the street as if he expected there to be trouble with each step he took. If something unexpected were to suddenly present itself he would be more than ready for it. He was a true professional in every sense of the word.

'Howdy, stranger,' Jim said when the man had reached where he was now leaning against the post.

The gunfighter looked him up and down. 'Sheriff,' he answered politely but without any degree of warmth.

'Looking for somewhere to stay?' Jim asked, guessing that the fellow was walking rather than riding to give himself the opportunity to better spot a boarding house he could bunk down in.

The man stopped walking and regarded Jim silently for a moment. 'As a matter of fact I am. Is there a problem with that?'

'Not with me there ain't,' Jim said amiably. 'What was wrong with taking a room at the saloon?'

The fellow seemed to relax. 'Too noisy,' he said. 'I like to turn in early and rise early. Can't get to sleep at night with all the noise that makes its way upstairs from the barroom when I stay in a saloon.'

'Luckily for you the saloon ain't the only place to stay in town.'

'Got any suggestions?'

'Larissa Johnson's place. Two-storey whitewashed house about two hundred yards further up the street. Clean rooms, fresh sheets on the bed, and good food.'

'Sounds like what I'm looking for. Much obliged to you.' He made to move off again.

'You wouldn't be looking for work would you?'

The stranger stopped and looked at Jim more closely this time. 'I reckon you know the kind of work I do, Sheriff.'

Jim nodded. 'And that's exactly the kind of work I'm offering you, only, you'd be on the right side of the law if you throw your lot in with me.'

'I take it you either have trouble in town you can't handle yourself or you've heard there's trouble on the way.'

'There's trouble on the way in the form of a man seeking revenge against folks in Caldwell. They dared to put him in prison more than twenty years back.'

'That's a mighty long time to bear a grudge.'

'He has a mighty long memory.'

'How many men does he have riding with him?'

'Six besides himself.'

'All gunfighters?'

'Yep.'

'And how many men are with you?'

'Just one who's any good with a gun.'

The stranger looked at Jim's bandaged hand. 'Not your gun hand I hope?'

'I'm afraid so.'

'Then you're up against it in a big way, aren't you,' he said, it being a statement rather than a question. 'What would make you think I'd be interested in throwing in with you?'

'Money . . . I'd see that you're paid real well.'

'A dead man has no use for money, and it seems I'd be deader than they come if I was to hire my gun out to you.'

'There's always the chance that could happen,' Jim agreed.

'More than a chance by the sounds of it.' He looked up the street for a moment before turning back to Jim. 'Whitewashed house, you said?'

'Yep.'

'A Mrs Larissa Johnson?'

'That's the lady.'

'I'm much obliged to you for pointing me in her direction, but I have to say no to the job offer.'

Jim's heart sank. He had really thought the fellow might be interested, but obviously he was not. 'I understand,' he said, without betraying the frustration he felt.

Jim watched with disappointment as the stranger carried on up the street in search of Larissa Johnson's boarding house. He just may have been an answer to Jim's prayers if he had been amenable to what he was being offered. But on the surface it did look like a fellow would have to be mad to go up against seven experienced gunman when all you had to back you up was one deputy and a crippled sheriff.

*

123

Wade Baxter himself came galloping into town later that afternoon; obviously the warning Jim had sent him via his men hadn't fazed him one iota. Trouble was about to erupt in the busy streets, and it would be trouble on a scale never seen before in Caldwell. A man tried and convicted for a crime he hadn't committed was here to exact revenge, and he wouldn't rest until his lust for blood had been quenched.

Jim wasn't sure how long it would be before Baxter began his campaign of retribution. Maybe he would leave it a day or two so he could find out who remained from that crowd who had sent him up for twenty-odd years. Maybe he would let them sweat awhile before he killed them. After all, revenge was sweetest when those you wished to punish could see their demise coming but were unable to do anything about it. It was Wade Baxter's game now, and Jim could do nothing more than wait and see how he wanted to play it.

If he had thought he had seen or heard the last of the gunfighter who had breezed into town earlier that day he was mistaken. A couple of hours before sundown he was standing at the door of the sheriff's office, a look of grim determination established on his unshaven face. 'Is that job offer still open, Sheriff?' he stepped across the threshold and entered the room. 'If it is I've changed my mind.'

Jim Sandford suppressed the urge to shout for joy. 'It sure is. I don't know how much it pays yet, I'll have to discuss it with the mayor and see what they're prepared to offer.'

The stranger brushed the comment off with a dismissive wave of his hand. 'I don't care about the money. Just pay me whatever you can afford. I'm doing this for other reasons.'

'Such as?'

'Three of those hombres riding with this Wade Baxter feller did me wrong in Abilene three years back and I've been wanting to put things to rights ever since. Those sons of. . . .' he looked at Jim for a moment, 'Well let's just say they've got something coming to them and I'd like to be the feller who gives it to them.'

Jim could see the cold rage behind those dark eyes and so decided the best policy would be to not press the matter any further. If this stranger wanted to get even with three of Baxter's men then that was all right with Jim Sandford. In fact, that was more than all right with him. There was nothing like a personal vendetta to spur a man on to taking another man down, and not even a big sum of money could motivate him as much as pure hatred could.

Reaching into his desk drawer, Jim pulled out a deputy's badge and tossed it to him. 'Pin that on. It'll make whatever you do to them legal.'

The fellow looked at the chunk of tin for a moment and grinned. 'I never thought I'd see the day I'd be wearing one of these things.'

'There's a first time for everything,' Jim said matter-of-factly.

'I'm pretty sure this will be the first and last time,' he attached the badge to his store-bought shirt and then turned to look at his reflection in the window. 'Almost looks like I'm the real thing,' he said dryly.

'For the time being you are. I'm Jim Sandford by the way.'

The stranger took the hand offered to him and proved his grip was just as strong as Jim's. 'Jeff Maddox.'

The name rang a bell with Jim. There had been a Jeff Maddox who had out-gunned the Breland brothers in a showdown in the main street of Denver a few years back. Jim hadn't been there to see it but he had heard the story from someone who had. Maddox had taken them both down without either managing to get a shot off. His reputation had only grown since. If there was one man Jim would want on his side in a crisis then it would be this man.

'Have you been sheriff of Caldwell for long?'

'Thirteen days.'

Maddox threw back his head and laughed like it was the first time he ever had. 'You sure know how to court trouble,' he said when he had recovered enough to speak. 'There are some lawmen who last ten years in the job and never see trouble like you're about to, but you come up against it after only thirteen days. If that ain't bad luck I don't know what is.'

Jim smiled at his comment. 'What can I say? I'm just a glutton for excitement.' It was the type of excitement he could do without, but he had run for office, won the election and accepted the appointment, so now he felt obliged to fulfil the role despite the fact it might cost him his life.

'So what's the plan where this Baxter feller is concerned?'

'I guess we have to wait and see what his next move is going to be. If he threatens anybody or does anything to harm anyone then we'll have to bring him in.'

'Which he won't do without a fight.'

'Which he won't do without a fight,' Jim agreed.

'And where's this deputy of yours right now? Shouldn't he be here with you now that Baxter and his men are in town?'

'He stepped out for a while to check on something.' Jim glanced up at the clock. 'That was over an hour ago. He should have been back by now.'

Maddox's left eyebrow went up a little. 'That sounds ominous.'

Now that he thought about it, Jim considered it to be a mite ominous, too. It wasn't like Bart to not be back when he said he would be, not when he was the punctual kind. 'Perhaps we'd better go and look for him,' Jim suggested as he got up from his chair and made for the door.

Outside, Caldwell was pretty much the same as it always was. Folks were still bustling here and bustling there just as if they had never heard of Wade Baxter, let alone that he was in their town planning to turn their whole world upside down. If Jim hadn't seen Wade Baxter and his men ride into town earlier, and hadn't known their intention for doing so, then he would have thought it was just business as usual in the small town.

'We'll try the mercantile first,' Jim said, hoping Bart had stopped off there to purchase some more tobacco and was either looking at what else was for sale or talking to Julia.

Julia Brooks looked up from her task of stacking cans of beans on a shelf when the two men walked in.

'Is Bart here?' Jim asked, casting his eye around the large store in an attempt to locate him.

'No, should he be?'

'I was hoping he might be.'

She picked up on his concern. 'Is Bart in some kind of trouble?'

'He might be,' Jim confessed, his fear for his friend and deputy going up another notch. 'He hasn't come back to the sheriff's office like I expected him to.'

Julia looked at the clock on the wall. 'He was in here about an hour ago if that helps any.'

'Did he say where he was heading to next?'

'He mentioned something about getting a new shoe put on his horse. One of them was coming loose, so he said.'

Jim relaxed a little. That was where he would be then, down at the smithy getting Ted Ryan to put a shoe on his mare. 'Thanks, Julia,' he made a move towards the door.

'Jim . . . can I have a quick word with you?'

'Wait for me outside,' he said to Maddox, 'I won't

be long.'

The gunfighter flashed him a knowing smile before disappearing outside to roll himself a cigarette and wait for his employer to join him.

'What's on your mind?' he asked the pretty woman.

She hesitated for a moment. 'It's just . . . what with all that's going on at the moment . . . this feud between Jake Westlake and Ethan Drake . . . and Pa says that it's dangerous for me to be seen with you at the moment. . . .'

Jim realized she was trying to justify why she was about to tell him she couldn't see him anymore and so saved her the trouble. 'You do what you think best, Julia. If that's not seeing me anymore then so be it.'

'It'll just be until all this trouble in Caldwell has blown over,' she said quickly. 'As soon as everything is back to normal we can go back to how we were.'

He looked coldly at her for a moment. 'We'll see,' he said quietly.

'Pa doesn' think I should get too attached to you in case. . . .' she stopped herself just in time.

'In case Wade Baxter and his men kill me?'

She didn't answer, just stared at the floor in front of her feet.

'It's a very real possibility, Julia.'

'You could hand in your badge then you would be safe.'

'But you wouldn't want me after that. Not when folks in town started saying that Jim Sandford is a coward. Besides, I've never run from a fight in my life and I don't intend to start now. If Wade Baxter wants a war I'll give him one.'

'I'm sorry things can't be different,' she said, still not lifting her eyes up to look at him.

'So am I, Julia, so am I.' Without saying another word Sheriff Jim Sandford turned and, striding to the door, left his long-time dream standing motionless on the mercantile shop floor, no doubt relieved she had extricated herself from a difficult situation with the minimum of fuss.

CHAPTER FIFTEEN

'He's been shot in the back,' Jim said as he carefully examined the barely breathing deputy lying on the ground behind the smithy. The blacksmith lay not five yards away in a pool of his own blood, his lifeless eyes staring up into the bright Kansas sun. 'They must have seen Bart come down here and decided to deal to him while he was without me to back him up.'

Maddox looked over the sheriff's shoulder as he examined the fallen deputy. 'It'll be Baxter and his men all right, doing all they can to remove any obstacle to their plans.'

'We need to get him to a doctor pronto. He's already lost a lot of blood. He can't afford to lose any more or he's got no hope of surviving this at all.'

Maddox nodded. 'Between the two of us we should be able to carry him.'

After Bart was safely ensconced at Doc Turner's house, Jim and Maddox headed back to the safety of the sheriff's office. Jim had what amounted to a crisis on his hands now. He had been relying on the fast gun of Bart Newcomb being available when the shooting started but now that option had been snuffed out. The doc seemed to think Bart would pull through but he wouldn't be any use to Jim in this particular fracas, and so now he was down to just Jeff Maddox.

They were barely back in the sheriff's office when Jim turned to Maddox. 'You can pull out if you want to and I'll not think any the worse of you. This is no longer the deal I promised you.'

'And let you have all the fun. No sirree, I'm in this all the way. Besides, it's like I told you, I've got a score to settle with three of those fellers.'

Jim felt a small measure of relief. 'There are a few men I can call on. John Anderson the gunsmith for one. He promised me he'd stand by me if I ever needed him to. Well, I need him to now. Then there's Blake, Clements, and Turnball. They all pledged their support to me as well.'

'Well now's the time to be calling on them I reckon. With one man dead and another in a bad way Baxter needs to be stopped before he goes on a rampage.'

'Right,' Jim said with conviction. 'You wait for me here and I'll be back in half an hour with enough men to wipe out that rat's nest down at the saloon.'

The bell on the gunsmith's shop tinkled out a dire warning for John Anderson as he looked up and saw who it was. Jim Sandford was the last man he wished to see right now, except maybe for Wade Baxter.

'John, I have a favour to ask of you,' Jim said before he had even closed the door behind him.

'I know what it is, Jim, and I'm afraid the answer has to be no,' Anderson said quickly. 'I'm no gunfighter.'

'You're a handy man with both a rifle and a scattergun, John, and that's all I'd need you to do. You wouldn't have to draw on anyone.'

John Anderson shook his head vigorously. 'The answer's still no.'

'What happened to your promise to back me up no matter what? I seem to remember you telling me that only one short week ago in this very store.'

'I didn't mean taking on gunfighters!' Anderson's voice went up a couple of pitches. 'I'll help you round up drunks and break up fights, but I'm not going to throw my life away.'

The shop door opened and Blake, Clements, and Turnball walked in.

'Am I glad to see the three of you,' Jim said, his heart beating nineteen to the dozen at the possibility they might renege on their offer of help, too.

Turnball glanced briefly at Jim before looking at Anderson. 'We're here to help John defend his shop if Baxter and his men try to break in and steal weapons, but nothing more.'

'The three of you said you'd help me out if I ever needed backing up,' Jim said, pretending he hadn't heard Turnball's remark. 'Well I sure do need it right now.'

'We ain't going up against Wade Baxter and his

men,' Turnball said firmly. 'There's only so much you can ask a man to do.'

'If you three don't help me then Baxter's gunna tear this town apart. Folks you've known all your life are gunna get killed. Doesn't that mean something to you?'

'In a situation like this it's every man for himself. You get paid to stop the likes of Wade Baxter and his men. So why don't you get out there and do your job?'

Jim finally lost his temper. 'You four sorry excuses for men make me sick to my stomach!' he yelled. 'I've known five-year-old boys with more guts than any of you have got.'

Jim Sandford left the gunsmith's shop before he did something he might regret. He would have had more respect for them if they had never pledged their support to him in the first place rather than to withdraw it when he was in most need. He stood on the boardwalk outside the gunsmith shop and considered his options. The town must have heard something had happened down at the smithy and now suspected it was about to happen out here in the street for there wasn't a single soul to be seen the length nor breadth of Caldwell. Shutters were being put up in the shop windows and closed signs hung on the doors. The good folks of Caldwell were expecting the worst and were doing all they could to shut themselves away from what was about to come, leaving Sheriff Jim Sandford to face the storm alone.

He hated to do it but there was no alternative. He

would have to go cap in hand to Sam Carrington. The ex-sheriff of Caldwell was his only hope now, and so with a heavy heart he made his way up the street to the little blue cottage, and then rapping urgently on the solid wood door waited impatiently for someone to answer.

'Hello, Amy,' he said meekly as Sam Carrington's wife of thirty years opened the door and glared at him with hatred in her pale blue eyes.

'What do you want?' she demanded coldly.

'I wondered if I could see Sam.'

'I don't think he wants to see you, young man!'

'Please, Amy, this is very important. People's lives are at stake.'

She considered his remark carefully for a while. 'I suppose if you must come in then you must,' she said with the same iciness she had displayed when she had opened the door to him.

Jim followed her through to the parlour, where she left him to his fate.

Sam Carrington looked up from his armchair to see who it was, and after the initial shock had worn off placed his newspaper on the small table beside him and fixed Jim with a malevolent glare. 'You've got a cheek coming here, boy!'

'Sam, there's serious trouble brewing. There are seven gunfighters in town and they aim to go on a killing spree that I can't stop on my own.' The words had just come spilling out of him. Sam Carrington had always been the man he had turned to in a crisis and the sight of him sitting there, a wise head resting on broad shoulders, made him feel like a small boy seeking guidance from his father.

Unfortunately for Jim, Sam Carrington was feeling anything but fatherly, and he was more than primed to let Jim know. 'You wanted this job,' he said, pointing an index finger in the younger man's direction, 'now you've got it. You can't go running scared the first time the going gets rough.'

'This thing is bigger than what's gone on between you and me, Sam. A lot of people are gunna get killed by Wade Baxter unless you and I do something to stop him.'

'We . . . you're dreaming if you think I'm gunna help the skunk who lost me my job.'

'Sam . . . you're not telling me you'd stand by and let innocent people get hurt simply because of a vendetta you have against me?'

'You took from me the only thing that meant anything to me. Fifteen years I served the township of Caldwell, merely to be cast aside by an upstart punk like all those years I gave were worth nothing. I owe this town and those who voted me out of office nothing, and I hope you get what's coming to you, Jim Sandford.'

There was going to be no help from his old mentor. Jim had humbled himself but had just been rejected in spectacular fashion. Not bothering to press the matter any further, he left Sam Carrington where he sat, retraced his footsteps to the front door as the older man's laughter floated along behind him, and then left the Carrington household never to return. He was halfway back to the sheriff's office when he was startled by a sudden burst of gunfire. There must have been half a dozen or so shots fired in quick succession. Taking cover behind a horse trough, he peered anxiously along the deserted street in an attempt to locate where the disturbance had originated from.

He didn't have long to wait. Within seconds several men spilled out of the sheriff's office and high-tailed it back to the saloon. They were Wade Baxter's men, and that could only mean they had stormed the sheriff's office in Jim's absence. Breaking cover and sprinting for all he was worth, Jim made it to the door of the office without incident, stepped over two dead men and glanced frantically around until his eyes came to rest on a body lying on the floor in the corner of the room.

'Jeff . . .' he said quietly, hoping that his newfound friend was still alive. Crossing the room with trepidation, he rolled the gunfighter over and looked intently into his eyes.

'Sorry, Jim old boy,' Jeff Maddox said with difficulty, 'but it looks like you're gunna be on your own from here on in.'

'I should never have left you here on your own,' Jim said as he cradled the dying man in his arms. 'We should have stuck together to prevent something like this from happening.'

'Those three hombres I told you about. The three I wanted to get even with. They must have seen me ride into town and recognized me. They came for me, but I got two of them. But you're gunna have to get the last one for me. You will make sure you do won't you? He is the last one left amongst the three who killed my kid brother. He's wearing a blue shirt and a black sombrero.'

'I'll get him, Jeff; you have my word on that.'

It was as if the fellow had been hanging on just to hear Caldwell's sheriff make him that very promise, because no sooner had the words left Jim's lips then Jeff Maddox's eyes closed and his spirit lifted.

Lying him back down gently on the floor, Jim straightened up and looked around him. Three dead men littered the small room and before the hour was out there would be more corpses for the undertaker to deal with. One of them would most likely be Jim Sandford himself.

He was all alone now, and although Jeff had dealt with two of Wade Baxter's men before he stopped a load of lead himself, there was still Baxter and four men left, and it would only be a matter of time before they came to get him. His only hope was to do the unexpected and take the fight to them. They had just killed a duly appointed deputy sheriff so Jim had every right to bring them in, either dead or alive, and the alive bit had just ceased to be an option.

Not stopping long enough to think it through, as to do so might mean he would change his mind, Jim walked over to the gun-rack and selecting a double-barrelled shotgun, loaded it up and made for the door. He would duck through the alley beside the sheriff's office and emerge on the street forty or so yards away from the saloon. That way he could cross over and creep up to the batwings without being seen. He was about to give Wade Baxter and his boys a taste of their own medicine, and if he died while doing it then so be it.

Fifteen minutes later he had his back up against the front of the saloon, the babble of voices from Baxter's men drifting out to him as he inched his way towards the batwings, desperately hoping no one would step outside and raise the alarm.

He snuck a quick peep through the window and was relieved to see the barroom was empty of patrons. Caldwell's men folk had wisely skedaddled when Wade Baxter had requisitioned it for his headquarters. That meant when he started blasting away he wouldn't hit anyone but those who deserved to be hit. Ducking under the window, he scooted to the other side and, straightening up, resumed his painstaking progression towards those batwings and his ultimate fate.

He would just have time to discharge both barrels of his shotgun before the element of surprise wore off. After that it was anyone's guess how long he would survive before they cut him down in a hail of bullets.

Five more steps to the batwings . . . four . . . three . . . two . . .and then he was there, right beside them. Taking a deep breath he spun round and, stepping briskly through the swinging doors, levelled the shotgun at the group of men sitting at a table in the middle of the room. 'This is for what you did to Jeff!'

he shouted, and then pulled the first trigger.

A bearded man with black shoulder-length hair copped the full brunt of the blast in his chest, but not waiting to congratulate himself on his success Jim fired again, knocking a short stocky man who had leapt to his feet backwards across the table, the sudden thump of his heavy body on the flimsy table top snapping two of its legs and sending the man to the floor, with bottles and glasses flying in all directions. The man was wearing a blue shirt and a black sombrero.

The chaos Jim had just created gave him time to retreat back through the batwings and seek cover. Two more of Wade Baxter's men were down and now there were only three men left for Jim to worry about. He had just made it across the street and positioned himself behind a farm wagon when the plate glass window of the Lonely Bull Saloon shattered into a hundred or more pieces and Wade Baxter and his men began to return fire.

Jim hunkered down behind the wagon and waited the initial barrage out. He was still outnumbered, and by three experienced gunmen no less. He was going to have to do something pretty spectacular and mighty soon if he was going to swing the odds in his favour.

He happened to glance up at the top-storey window of the mercantile and spotted Julia and her father watching the event unfold in the street below. It would be so easy for Harrison Brooks to train a rifle on the saloon from there and keep them pinned down. But it appeared he was more than content to leave Jim to his fate, and if the impassive look on Julia's face was anything to judge by then so was she.

Baxter and his men had abandoned the use of their six-guns and were now employing rifles, and the effect they were having on the brittle timber of the old farm wagon was devastating. With great chunks of wood being carved off at regular intervals, Jim had the nous to realize that if he stayed where he was for much longer then that was where he would draw his final breath. Feeding two more cartridges into the shotgun, Jim Sandford readied himself for a near-suicidal dash for safety.

Lying on his stomach and rolling clear of the wagon, Jim let go with both barrels consecutively, the first load of buckshot splintering the batwings to matchwood, while the second roared in through the broken window, forcing Baxter and his men to duck down out of sight. It gave Jim the precious seconds he needed to leap to his feet and dart down the street to find better cover. If Baxter wanted him dead he would have to come after him, and to do that he would have to leave the relative safety of the saloon. Jim hoped the outlaw wanted him dead badly enough to attempt it. Out here on the street Jim had a chance if he turned the conflict into a running battle. He just had to make sure he didn't stay too long in one place. Keeping Wade Baxter guessing as to Jim's whereabouts was the key to success.

A full rain barrel on the corner of the milliner's caught his eye and so he abandoned his flight and gratefully crouched down behind it. He only had thirty seconds or so up his sleeve before he saw one of Baxter's men making his way stealthily up the street towards him, using every obstacle from horse troughs to buggies to shop doorways to avoid getting better acquainted with lead from Jim's scattergun.

Jim reloaded. At the moment his trusty shotgun seemed to be the best weapon to be using, but he knew that sooner or later it would come down to using his Colt, and that meant getting up close and personal with his enemy, something that he was loathe to do with his busted up fingers and knuckles forcing him to shoot with his left hand. Accuracy at that close range was all important with a six-gun, and Jim feared he just might not have what it took if it came down to a stand-up shootout.

The man inching his way up the street hadn't seen Jim go to ground. Jim could see him looking frantically all around in a desperate attempt to locate where the man he was after was hidden. Jim decided to keep himself tucked well down out of sight until he could get a fatal shot sent in his direction. He didn't have to wait long, the fellow might be good with a gun but he was short on patience, and so all of a sudden he abandoned the water trough he had been crouching behind and came bounding down the boardwalk with the type of recklessness that only a man of his tender years could possess.

Jim Sandford couldn't believe his luck. If the fellow had wanted to throw his life away then he couldn't have done it any easier than how he was

142

going about it now. He must have thought the coast was clear and that Jim was further down the street. But he was soon to find out to his detriment that he was very much mistaken.

The youngster was twelve yards away when Jim popped up and gave him a full load of buckshot. The force of the lead hitting his body lifted him off his feet and threw him several feet backwards, bringing him to rest on his back on the boardwalk. His body was wracked by one prolonged spasm before it finally lay still, a pool of blood seeping slowly down to drip off the end of the boardwalk and onto the street.

Jim had almost turned this whole thing around. Despite the fact he had been forsaken by every able-bodied man in town he had taken this from being impossible to being a good chance he was going to win this contest. There was only Wade Baxter and one other man left to deal to and then the threat to Jim and the township of Caldwell would be snuffed out.

He had just straightened up when he heard the click of a hammer being cocked from somewhere just behind him.

'You've done well, Sheriff, but all good things must come to an end.'

Turning around very slowly, Jim looked into the eyes of a man in his early thirties, clean shaven, hatless with closely cropped blond hair; he bore the self-satisfied smile of a man who knew he was just about to win.

'And you are?' Jim asked in a cavalier fashion,

hoping to stall the fellow long enough so he could figure a way out of this predicament.

'Your worst nightmare. If you're a praying man I suggest you get on to it quick cos you ain't got much longer left to live.'

Jim contemplated his options. He still had the shotgun in his hands but both barrels were now empty. He could let it drop and reach for his Colt but he would have to clear leather faster than any man ever had before to beat the cocked gun in the fellow's hand. Besides, he would be using his left hand, which would put him at a decided disadvantage anyway. This was certainly beginning to look like the end of the road for Jim Sandford, sheriff of Caldwell.

He wondered what they would put on his tombstone. Would it say something like 'Here lies James Bryan Sandford, who died in the line of duty', or would it just have his name and date of death? It was ironic that such a thing was running through his mind at a moment like this, the moment before he died, but then the whole thing seemed surreal anyway, as if it were merely a dream and he would wake up soon and laugh at the silliness of it all.

'That's enough time to make your peace with God,' the fellow said. 'Now you get to meet him.'

There was a loud boom, and hundreds of shards of glass flew across the boardwalk to the left of Jim and showered the man. But it wasn't the glass that made him drop his six-gun, nor was it the reason he hit the dust of the street and failed to get up, no, it was the roar of fiery lead from a shotgun fired through the barber's shop window that did the damage. The suddenness of it all left Jim dazed for a few seconds, and when he was finally back in control of all his faculties he looked to see who his saviour was.

'I couldn't leave you to cope with this on your own,' Ruth said through the opening where only seconds ago a plate glass window emblazoned with 'Johansson's Barber Shop' had taken pride of place. 'I just couldn't let him kill you when I knew I could stop him.'

'You've been incredibly brave,' he said gently, smiling at her with true admiration in his heart.

'Let me help you get Baxter.'

He could see she meant it, too. 'You have done plenty already, Ruth. You have just saved my life and evened up the odds for me. It's come down to just me and Wade Baxter now, and for the first time since the shooting started I'm feeling optimistic that it'll be me who's still standing when the smoke clears.'

'But two of us will stand a better chance,' she argued.

He could see she was beginning to tremble. She had never killed a man before and so the realization that she had just done that very thing was only now beginning to affect her. What she needed was to get right away from here to where she would be safe. Baxter was still at large, and he wouldn't be happy that his plans had been thwarted by a lone sheriff and a young girl. She was in danger if she went with

Jim and she was in danger if she stayed where she was right now.

'You must go somewhere you'll be safe,' he urged her.

'But what about you?'

'I'll be all right,' he promised her, even though he had no right to make such a promise. Wade Baxter was a very dangerous man and quite capable of figuring out how to come out on top in this conflict. 'I will worry about you if you stay here. You must go somewhere you'll be safe, Ruth.'

'If you think it best, Jim,' he noted the disappointment in her voice, but really it was her safety that was paramount to him. He would never forgive himself if she got killed while trying to defend him.

'I will go out the back door and then up the street to Alice Cartwright's place. It's only a few minute's walk from here. I'll be safe there.'

'I will come and see you when this is over.'

She smiled, but there were tears in her pretty eyes. Then without another word passing between them she turned and made her way to the back door of the barber's shop.

Jim headed back towards the saloon. He suspected that was where he would find Wade Baxter. He would have sent his last men out to deal with the troublesome sheriff and waited until their successful return before going on the rampage through Caldwell that would satiate his lust for revenge.

Jim had walked less than sixty yards from the barber's shop when he heard a shout from behind him. Spinning around with his hand clasping the butt of his Colt, he tried to make out where it had come from.

A man stepped down off the boardwalk not far from where Jim had left Ruth; he was pushing a woman in front of him.

'I've got your woman, Sandford,' he yelled, his voice carrying on the still air as clearly as if he were standing right in front of Jim.

'Dang it!' Jim's heart lurched. 'I should have taken her to Alice Cartwright's myself.'

Baxter must have exited through the back of the saloon and come across Ruth as she was making her way to Alice's. No doubt he had heard the gunshot, saw his man lying in the street and Ruth standing on the boardwalk talking to Jim and come to the conclusion she meant something to him. Now he had her, and for the first time Jim realized how much she really did mean to him. If she didn't then he wouldn't be feeling so full of fear for her right now.

'You've been a thorn in my side, Sandford,' Baxter continued, pushing the girl ahead of him as he prodded the barrel of a six-gun into her back.

Dropping the shotgun, Jim cautiously retraced his steps back down the street towards them.

'I had everything worked out, and if you hadn't interfered I would have left you alone. There were others in Caldwell I planned to punish for what they did to me and you weren't one of them.'

This was something Jim hadn't figured on. He had fully expected it to come down to a shootout between him and Baxter, but not with Ruth being used as a pawn in the proceedings.

'But now you've made me mad, Sandford, and I'm an ornery cuss when I get my dander up.'

Jim's mind raced. How could he get Baxter to let Ruth go?

'You're gunna have to pay for your interference. No man crosses me and gets away with it. I have a long memory when it comes to those who give me grief. Just ask some of the citizens of this town.'

They were forty yards apart now and the gap closing.

'I'm afraid I'm gunna have to hurt your little woman. You see, that'll hurt you where it counts, and hurting you means more to me than anything just at the moment, I'm so hopping mad at you.'

He would hurt her, too, Jim knew that he would. There was no honour in the man, not a scrap of chivalry or decency to be found. He would harm Ruth for no other reason than to cause Jim pain.

'What's it gunna feel like when I blow her brains out the side of her head,' Baxter said coldly. 'Are you gunna scream out her name as her lifeless body drops down into the dust and dirt of this sorry little street?'

The man was evil itself. He was glorying in his moment of power, revelling in the fear he was evoking not just in his captive but in the man standing opposite him. All those years of prison hadn't changed him for the better. He was a bitter and sadistic man, hell bent on gratifying his warped sense of

148

justice through the use of violence.

'The woman means nothing to me, Baxter,' Jim lied, hoping he would let her go but suspecting it would be nothing short of a miracle if he did.

'Are you sure about that?' Cocking back the hammer on his pistol and pressing it against the side of her head, he grinned broadly.

The distance between them was down to thirty yards now.

'Why don't you just behave like a man and we'll have this out between the two of us. Me against you right here in the street? The girl doesn't need to come into it.'

'Oh but she does. I want you to see her die before I kill you. I want you to bawl like a baby when you watch me take her life away from her. That would be the ultimate revenge.'

'And revenge is what you live for isn't it, Baxter?' Jim said in disgust.

'You can bet your last silver dollar it is. For more than twenty years I paid for a crime I didn't commit because the people of this town convinced a court of law I had committed it. I've had plenty of time not only to hate them for what they did to me but to plan how I was going to pay them back. And now I'm here to see that through, but you've poked your nose in and messed it all up for me.'

His voice had gone up a couple of pitches. Wade Baxter was getting angrier by the second.

'You mightn't have committed the crime you got put away for, Baxter, but you had committed plenty of crimes you deserved to be punished for but weren't.'

Jim was only fifteen feet away now, and he could see the terror in Ruth's eyes as the madman who held her from behind twisted the barrel of his pistol savagely into her temple.

'You're just begging me to blow her brains out,' Baxter screamed, 'and they say I'm the crazy one.'

Jim knew he had no more than thirty seconds to turn this around and save Ruth's life before Baxter squeezed that trigger and sent her off to her reward.

CHAPTER SIXTEEN

Jim's eyes made contact with Ruth's. The look that passed between them conveyed all that the young woman needed to know about what Jim Sandford was about to do. If she played her part just right then maybe she would walk away from this.

Jim directed his eyes to a spot over Baxter's right shoulder and suddenly yelled, 'No don't!'

Wade Baxter's reflexes kicked in, as he instantly craned his head around to look for the non-existent threat the barrel of his pistol came away from Ruth's temple and so she bent her head forward to give Jim a better chance of delivering a fatal shot.

Jim Sanford's Colt leapt out of his holster courtesy of his left hand, and working the hammer back with his thumb he took only as much time as he dared to aim at the outlaw's head before he pulled the trigger, the bullet hitting Baxter in the face just as he realized the sheriff's shout was a bluff and had flicked his eyes back to the lawman. Releasing his grip on the young woman, he took a couple of backward steps as he tried to comprehend what had just happened.

Jim took advantage of his enemy's lapse in concentration and, cocking the hammer back on his Colt, waited until Ruth was well clear before taking careful aim and pulling the trigger for the second time.

Wade Baxter grunted loudly when the bullet hit him this time, his chest suddenly experiencing a burning pain that ripped all the way through to his shoulder blades. 'You . . . you . . .' in his fury he tried to raise his six-gun but the effort was too much for him, and within seconds it had slipped from his grasp and lay silently at his feet, never to be the cause of a man's death again.

A bubbling gurgle rushed up through Baxter's throat as he expelled bright red blood over the front of his clean white shirt, then taking a few wobbling steps forward, he sank first to his knees then pitched face forward onto the street no more than ten feet away from Jim.

Ruth rushed straight into Jim's arms the moment she was sure Baxter wasn't going to get up. 'I'm so glad he didn't kill you,' she said, valiantly stifling the sobs that were trying to take control of her as she realized how close she had come to losing her own life.

'It's me who should be saying that to you.' He looked down at the dead man. 'He won't be troubling anyone in Caldwell now, or anywhere else for that matter.'

Ruth's mother came rushing up the street frantically calling her daughter's name.

152

'It's all right, Ma,' Ruth assured her when the older woman had joined her and Jim, 'neither Jim nor I are hurt.'

'Thank you,' Harriet Matheson said to Jim before she took her daughter by the hand and led her through the crowd that had spilled out of the buildings on either side of the street. They had begun to gather around the body of Wade Baxter to stare at the man who had only minutes earlier struck such fear into every citizen in Caldwell who knew what he was capable of doing to them.

'I knew we had chosen the right man for the job,' John Anderson said as he came up and placed a hand on Jim's shoulder.

Jim Sandford stared into the gunsmith's eyes with cold indifference, then pushing past him endured the back slaps and congratulations as he forged his way through the men, women, and children who had brought the deserted street back to life. With a rising sense of anger born of disgust, he strode to the sheriff's office to see to the body of his fallen deputy.

Jim had spent a dream-free night sleeping deeply on a cot in one of the cells. He hadn't bothered to return last night to the room at the boarding house he had rented for the past few years. After he had helped the undertaker with the bodies of Baxter's men, and seen Jeff Maddox decently buried as well, he had scrubbed the blood off the floor of the sheriff's office and then, with exhaustion gripping his entire body, staggered through to that cot and

153

gratefully laid his big frame down on it. He hadn't woken up until the sun peeped through the barred window up above his head. Swinging his long legs over the side of the cot, he planted his feet firmly on the stone floor and yawned. It was then that the events of the previous day came flooding back to him. He had never killed a man before but he had yesterday. He had killed several men in fact, and the knowledge of that saddened him. Baxter and his men deserved to die because they planned to kill innocent people, but that didn't make it sit any easier with Jim Sandford. Getting off the cot, he made his way out to the office to brew some coffee.

Jim heard them before he saw them. An excited babbling array of male voices drifted down the street towards the open door of the sheriff's office. Jim Sandford groaned. He just knew they were coming to see him.

Two minutes later his fear was realized as more than a dozen men trooped in through the door to stand in front of the desk Jim was sitting at, trying to enjoy his second cup of morning coffee.

'Jim Sandford, we're here to congratulate you on a job well done and to inform you that you have our full support in your role as sheriff of this town.'

Placing his coffee cup down on the desk, Jim looked the mayor of Caldwell up and down. He was dressed in all his mayoral finery as if this was the greatest of occasions.

'I didn't have your support yesterday,' he answered with a chilliness that wasn't lost on them. 'Not a single man among you had the guts to make a stand alongside me. The whole lot of you forsook me. It took a woman to come to my rescue.'

The mayor's eyes took on a hurt look. 'If you had given us some time to prepare. . . .'

'Balderdash!' Jim exclaimed loudly.

'I can assure you it isn't,' the stunned mayor said. 'We would every man of us have helped you if you had only presented us with a workable plan we could have followed.'

'You followed the only workable plan men of your calibre know,' Jim said sourly. 'That was keeping yourself well hidden until it was all over.'

'I had my gun strapped on and was about to join you when I got word that you had already taken care of everything,' the mayor protested. 'It was all over so quickly none of us had a chance to do anything to help you.'

Jim stabbed a finger at him in fury. 'Don't you come into my office spouting your ballyhoo trying to bamboozle me, you strutting little peacock!'

Shock registered on the older man's face. He had never been subjected to disrespect like this before, and to think that he had not only voted for the young upstart in the election that had ousted Sam Carrington, but he had been the one who had pushed him to stand in the first place.

'I realize you went through quite an ordeal yesterday but that doesn't give you the right to speak to me or those who are with me so rudely,' the mayor said in rather a haughty fashion.

Jim slowly drew himself up to his full height and glared down at the top official in the township of Caldwell. 'I'll do a dang sight more'n speak rudely, you pompous little man. I'll kick your fat butt out of this office and down the entire length of Caldwell if you aren't out of here in five seconds flat.'

'Well!' the mayor said indignantly. 'I have never been spoken to in such a manner in all my life. Maybe we need to rethink whether or not you really are the right person for the job of sheriff.'

Jim skirted round the table to join the mayor. 'Let me give you a hand to think it through before you make a decision on that, shall I. Or should I say let me give you a foot.'

Not being slow on the uptake the mayor was already beating a hasty retreat to the door when Jim's size thirteen foot caught him flush on his well-padded bottom.

'Of all the effrontery!' the mayor said loudly, quickening his pace so as to avoid a repeat performance from Caldwell's sheriff.

'I'd let you have it on the frontery as well if I could, but you're skedaddlin' so fast I'll have to be content with giving you another on your behindery,' Jim said gleefully as he delivered an even swifter kick to the man's hindquarters.

Jim Sandford stood in the doorway and laughed until his sides ached as he watched the man and his minions scurry up the street to seek safety from the sheriff, whom they considered had lost all control. He was glad to see them go. They were nothing more than a pack of cowardly hypocrites who had let him down badly. As he watched the last of them disappear into a building further up the street he knew what it was he must do. Grabbing his Stetson and gun-belt off the peg beside the door, he stepped through the opening and headed towards the boarding house to gather up what little belongings he had.

'Jim!' Ruth said in surprise when she answered the door to the ranch house later that afternoon.

'Ruth, I've come to say goodbye,' Jim said without fanfare.

Her face fell. 'Where are you going?'

'I thought my dream was to be a sheriff but I've discovered like Sam Carrington did that it's a thankless task, and when the chips are down those who should be backing you up don't. So I'm going to find a little spread somewhere and raise some beef. Build it up slowly until I've got something I'm proud of. I don't know where that will be yet but I figure I'll know the place when I see it.'

'Take me with you,' she said suddenly and without a hint of shame.

The suddenness of the suggestion took him by surprise, leaving him speechless.

'You must know that I've always loved you.'

He nodded. 'I suppose I did.'

'Then take me with you.'

'I would have to marry you to do that. I'm not the sort of man to take a woman and not put my ring on her finger.'

'Then marry me,' she said bluntly.

'Just like that?'

'Well it isn't quite that simple. You have to ask me to be your wife first.'

All thoughts of a life with Julia had gone from his head a couple of days ago. He had put Julia Brooks on a pedestal that she hadn't belonged on, and now that he looked at the young and loyal woman standing in front of him he was glad that those thoughts had gone. 'Ruth Matheson . . . will you marry me?'

'Yes I will, Jim Sandford, and I will make you a good wife, you just see if I don't.'

'How long will it take for you to get ready to travel?' he asked.

She smiled at him. 'About five minutes.'

As she and her mother bustled about and got her things together, Jim decided they would head from here to the livery stables, where he would buy a gig off the livery man. They would travel on to the next town, where he and Ruth would get married the first opportunity they got.

When Ruth met him at the door several minutes later it was with her mother in tow. 'With Pa dead and me gone Ma doesn't want to live here on her own. Can she come with us?'

Jim smiled. Harriet Matheson was an older version of her daughter. Jim had no objection whatsoever. 'I would be happy to have you come with us, Harriet,' he said tenderly.

'Ma said she is going to put the ranch up for sale

and we'll use the money to buy another one else-where, just the three of us."

Jim wasn't about to argue with the logic in that. He didn't have enough money to buy a ranch of his own, and wouldn't for several years, so this was a happy turn up for the books if ever there was one.

An hour later they were walking side by side down the main street of Caldwell, Ruth's mother trotting along behind with a happy smile on her face, when Julia Brooks stepped out of the mercantile and cast a cold eye in their direction.

'Good day to you, Miss Brooks,' Jim said in a formal manner, touching his finger to the brim of his Stetson, 'and I sincerely hope you have a happy life.'

Julia tossed her head as if to say 'good riddance'. No doubt she had just heard about his shameful conduct where the mayor was concerned and felt to be associated with him would merely bring shame to both her and her father.

As they left her behind Jim suddenly realized he was still wearing his badge so, halting, he plucked it from his shirt and, staring at it for a moment, tossed it into the horse trough beside him, watching it flash in the sun for the briefest of moments until it sank down into the murky depths of the stagnant water. It perfectly reflected his career as sheriff of Caldwell. He had shone brightly for the briefest of moments also, only to disappear without a trace.

'Let's leave this sorry little town far behind, Ruth,' he said lovingly, 'and promise each other we'll never mention its name again.' He kissed her then, knowing that he had finally found what was more important to him than the title of sheriff, and that was the love of a loyal woman.